PRAISE FROM REAL COPS FOR TOM PHILBIN AND HIS PREVIOUS NOVELS

"Rings absolutely true."
FRANK PUELLO, N.Y.P.D.
62nd Precinct

"Grippingly real, outstanding."
JOHN CARLTON, N.Y.P.D.
Retired

"Filled with mutts, maniacs, and mayhem—
just like I remember!"
BLAKE WILLIAMS, N.Y.P.D.
Retired

Also by Tom Philbin
Published by Fawcett Books:

PRECINCT: SIBERIA
UNDER COVER
COP KILLER
A MATTER OF DEGREE
JAMAICA KILL
STREET KILLER
DEATH SENTENCE
THE PROSECUTOR

DART MAN

Tom Philbin

FAWCETT GOLD MEDAL • NEW YORK

Sale of this book without a front cover may be unauthorized. If this book is coverless, it may have been reported to the publisher as "unsold or destroyed" and neither the author nor the publisher may have received payment for it.

A Fawcett Gold Medal Book
Published by Ballantine Books
Copyright © 1994 by Tom Philbin

All rights reserved under International and Pan-American Copyright Conventions. Published in the United States of America by Ballantine Books, a division of Random House, Inc., New York, and simultaneously in Canada by Random House of Canada Limited, Toronto.

Library of Congress Catalog Card Number: 93-91028

ISBN 0-449-14672-3

Manufactured in the United States of America

First Edition: May 1994

10 9 8 7 6 5 4 3 2 1

Chapter 1

Linda Wolosky, dressed in a tight red dress and black pumps, stood sideways and viewed herself in the long mirror secured to the back of the closet door.

At age twenty-three, Linda was completely satisfied with her body. Her breasts were not large, but her buttocks and legs were show stoppers. She was built like an Olympic ice skater. She had often thought that if she had her druthers, she would rather have a behind and legs like she had than large breasts. She knew that large breasts had a way of turning to fat, while legs and derrieres stayed solid and shapely for years. Her own mother could still turn heads.

Linda liked to show her body, and now, mid-July, she was out on the beach every chance she got. She wore only bikinis, and was well aware that to some degree she was an exhibitionist. After years of being ashamed of her body, she figured she was allowed that.

Linda was in her apartment in the Fordham Heights section of the Bronx. It wasn't a very good neighborhood, but the violence was generally restricted to drug dealers and their customers. She felt some measure of safety, since she shared the apartment with two other girls. June, like her, was a secretary in Manhattan, and Pat was a receptionist in a dentist's office.

Linda left the apartment around eight A.M. on Monday morning. She walked across Fordham Road, as she did every workday, to the IND stop at Fordham and the Concourse, rather than take the closer stop on the IRT elevated train. She got little extra exercise, and it refreshed her.

It was a particularly beautiful day, unseasonably cool, and she felt very good as she strode briskly across Fordham, a broad multilane street lined by all kinds of stores, from big department stores to tiny luncheonettes. She was thinking about her boyfriend, Ray, and the great time they had this past weekend at City Island, swimming and taking in the sun. There were at least three or four more good weekends left in the summer. It was exciting to look forward to.

The small black man with bloodshot eyes had been prowling the Fordham area for about an hour. He was looking for a certain kind of woman. He had an image in his mind: dark hair, dark-eyed, a sluttish figure, a certain kind of ass. He saw a number of women he would like to have fired at. They made him very angry. They wiggled their big asses, challenging him with them.

A couple of times he had gotten close enough to fire, but had not. There were too many people around. If he were seen, he might get caught. This was an area where people swiped gold necklaces, and it was not unusual for someone to take off after a chain snatcher. He could not run as fast as he once did.

No, he would pick someone he could do it to, and get away—to do it again as often as he liked.

He spotted her coming out of her building and followed her east on Fordham Road. She was wearing a red dress and had a sharply curved ass that swung back and forth as she walked.

He felt murderous. She was such a whore, such a bitch. And she flaunted it. Where he came from, they used to take sluts like this and throw them into a volcano.

Now, he could only do this.

Traffic on Fordham Road was heavy, but he was lithe and fast and he got across easily. Soon he was walking about fifteen yards behind her, watching her ass move, lock, and release, mocking him.

He would like to have hit her over the head with an ax. Or chop it off.

Instead he reached into the pocket of the checked sport jacket he was wearing.

His fingers touched the sturdy plastic straw. The dart was already loaded into it. He had been using the homemade gun for two months now, and he used the same kind of thing when he was a kid, so he was good at it. Accurate. He knew he could put the dart anyplace he wished. He knew where he wished.

The street was crowded. He closed the gap and was within five yards of her. He was sweating heavily. His eyes flicked around. It was time—and then it wasn't. As he was about to fire, someone came between himself and the whore, and then she was heading down the stairs to the subway, her heels clicking.

He followed.

Down in the tunnel it was cool and he could hear the sounds of trains. He was focused on her behind.

He stayed five yards behind her, waiting for a chance. But there were people everywhere—it was too risky to chance a shot. He was getting very nervous. Maybe he wouldn't get an opportunity.

She stood on line for tokens, and he also got on line.

As she waited, she turned idly this way and that. She was heavily made-up. Her ass jutted. She thought she was hot shit. She treated him like shit.

She bought several tokens while he bought just one.

She went through the turnstiles and he followed.

His chance would come. It must come. He would follow her onto the train, if necessary.

Soon they were standing on the crowded downtown subway platform. She stood a few feet back from the platform edge. He peeked at her ass from the side. It was a sharply curved, challenging, big whore ass. He was mesmerized and revolted by it.

As he looked, she glanced idly his way and he flushed with fear. He looked down. But she had looked right through him. He kept his head down awhile, then looked up. She was looking away from him in the direction the train would come.

The tracks clicked and then clanked. A downtown train was on its way.

The sound got louder and louder, and then the train hammered into the station. Instinctively, everyone backed away from the edge of the platform, including Linda Wolosky. He did not.

The train ground to a stop. It sounded like thousands of knives and forks being dumped on the tracks.

He tried to angle for a shot, but couldn't get one. People were pushing and shoving onto the train. There was no way he was going to get on without pushing himself in.

He had almost decided to look for her tomorrow, when a golden opportunity presented itself. Linda Wolosky had pushed herself onto the train, but her behind was facing out.

During that quiet moment just before the doors slid shut, he blew the dart expertly and angrily. It spiraled across the eight feet and smacked into her right buttock. Her head snapped back and her hand touched the spot just as the doors closed.

The man watched the commotion through the windows as the train pulled out of the station. He felt power, and sexual release. He loved it.

CHAPTER 2

Captain Warren Bledsoe, a bald, heavyset man who resembled Ed Asner, sat at his desk in a corner office on the first floor of the 53rd Precinct and looked aggrieved. It was noontime on Thursday and, thus far, the day could only be described as a shit sandwich. This was a typical day at the Five Three, better known as Fort Siberia. This precinct was filled with problems—it had the highest murder and robbery rates in the city. What's more, many of the cops had been exiled to Siberia because they had screwed up, or were generally incompetent, or were insubordinate, or alcoholics, or suspected of being thieves, or were hardheads or were psychotic enough to want the action. Bledsoe himself had been banished there for instigating a failed coup down at One Police Plaza, "The Ivory Tower," where all the brass was located.

His bad day had started in the early morning, due to his wife, whom he talked to as little as possible. Within two years of their marriage thirty-two years earlier, she had doubled in size and their relationship had gone downhill from there. The last time they had sex was the night Hubert Humphrey had announced his candidacy for president. They had no kids, but she had a dog, a little terrier who hated him and had left a surprise for his bare feet on more than one occasion.

The day before, Bledsoe's wife had started on one of her latest diets, this one having garlic as its central food, and when he had returned to their Riverdale home at around midnight—after a stomach-churning day at Fort Siberia—he became alarmed because he thought there was a gas leak in the apartment, until he realized that the smell was garlic, and that it was from his wife simply going about the business of breathing.

He had spent the whole night in fear that she would

fart, but she didn't. And he had more of the same to look forward to tonight.

Upon arrival at the precinct at eight, his aide, Sergeant Ray Fletcher, told him that there had been reports of a "disturbance" at a Korean fruit and vegetable market on Tremont Avenue, a confrontation between blacks and Koreans that was heating up. Fletcher said that he already got a call from Simon Parker, the fat black activist who spent $3000 a year having his hair done. Bledsoe knew Parker would be followed by one or more of those wacko attorneys who regarded all white men as mortal enemies.

Bledsoe had just completed a sigh over that when his intercom buzzed. He picked up the phone.

"Yeah?"

"Deputy Commissioner Slaughter on the phone," Fletcher said.

Bledsoe took a deep breath. Shit. Slaughter never called unless he had problems for him.

"Put him through."

"Bledsoe?"

"Yes sir, Chief, this is Captain Bledsoe. How can I help you?"

"I see that you had another Dart Man hit on Monday."

"Yes."

"Well, we just had another on 42nd Street about twenty minutes ago. What are you doing about your two?"

Bledsoe thought: Nothing. Absolutely nothing. Who gave a fuck about a guy shooting homemade darts in women's asses when he had half the fucking precinct shooting bullets at each other? The media talked about the needles—the guy used sewing needles and paper feathers—possibly being contaminated with the AIDS virus, but the guy had already attacked about thirty fucking women and there was no AIDS, and even if the needles were contaminated, the chances of getting AIDS was like one in a hundred, and none of the women ended up in ICU from a needle prick. It was a tempest in a teapot.

But Bledsoe was sensitive to inquiries from One Police Plaza even if they were unrelated to reality.

"I have some people looking into it, sir," he said.

"Any results?"

"Not yet, sir."

"Yeah, well, having a nutcase like that running around your precinct doesn't do anyone any good."

In his head, Bledsoe translated Slaughter's words. They meant that the media was making the brass look bad on this, and this translated into a negative mark for Bledsoe, who hoped to one day leave Siberia for something safer—say downtown Beirut.

"Well," Slaughter continued, "the PC is announcing today the formation of a task force to hunt the Dart Man, and he wants a man from every precinct affected. In other words, any precinct where there's been an assault. Do you have such a man? We're looking for a top investigator."

"Yes sir," Bledsoe said, and thought: It's such baloney. Another task force deal to pull the wool over the public and media eyes. All sound and fury signifying nothing.

"I'd like his name on my desk by tomorrow."

"Yes sir, I'll get right on it."

They hung up, and Bledsoe thought: So this son of a bitch wants me to assign a man in the precinct to a bullshit case that's just going to waste my time—and lower case clearance figures simply because that man won't be here.

A bullshit case, but one he could not ignore.

He picked up the phone.

"Yes sir," Fletcher said.

"Get me Joe Lawless," Bledsoe said, referring to the head of his Felony Squad.

"Yes sir," Fletcher said.

CHAPTER 3

George Benton felt good, which for him had been a fairly unusual state over the last few years. He was calm, relatively optimistic. He only thought about dying a few times a day. Love did that. It allowed you to look on the horizon and see red sails in the sunset instead of warships bearing down on you.

George, a detective First Grade in the Five Three, had been in pretty bad shape for a few years. In fact, four years ago, and four hours after his ex-wife's lawyer called to announce that she was divorcing him, he had a nervous breakdown and had spent six months in South Oaks Psychiatric Hospital, held together with drugs that, an aide said, "once in your bloodstream, would allow you to watch the *Titanic* go down with the same interest level you would have when eating a plate of mashed potatoes."

When he left the hospital he was still on Haldol, a powerful tranquilizer, but then he was called on to look into a series of serial murders, on which he was something of an expert, and he had gone off Haldol and succeeded in clearing it. It was just the boost—the bridge—his ego needed. In coming to understand the killer, he had come to understand something of himself, and had started psychotherapy—psychoanalysis—with a Dr. Morris Stern in Manhattan.

George went at least two times a week, sometimes three, if the job allowed. Though it was brutal, the anxiety almost unbearable at times, it increased his hope, and he started to understand some of the forces that had tortured him all his life.

And then, two years into therapy, he had met Dr. Ellen Stevens, a psychologist at Bellevue Hospital.

Benton had attended a series of her lectures on "Crime Scene and Profile Characteristics of Organized and Disorganized Murderers," which was about how you could profile serial murderers based on different crime scenes. Benton found the lectures—and her—fascinating. She was thirty-eight, a pretty, dark-haired, dark-eyed widow with a nice figure. Before she was halfway through her first lecture, she was doing strange things to George's stomach.

George was terrified of a new involvement with a woman, but he couldn't help himself. While very astute, she was also warm and caring, nonjudgmental. She had enormous empathy—even for the killers. He found himself falling in love. Not one of the four lectures went by without George standing up and asking her questions or engaging in dialogue. He loved talking to her, just loved having her look at him. The questions were a bonus.

He found the courage to ask her out, and she accepted. And his perception of her, and his love, was solidified the first time they made love. Or, rather, George didn't. He simply couldn't maintain an erection, a problem he had had with his first wife, who would get frustrated and angry about it. But Ellen didn't care.

"I hear about it all the time," she had said, "and it's not something to worry about. When you're ready, you'll do it. Anyway, it's not the basis of our relationship. I care for you because you're warm, loving, caring, understanding—and you turn me on, too."

Soon, swathed in her love and understanding, he was able to perform without any problems whatsoever, because he didn't feel like he was performing. He was making love.

George was in his three-room apartment—now their apartment—on Pelham Bay Parkway in the Bronx at around one-thirty on the same day that Slaughter had spoken to Captain Bledsoe. He was in the process of getting dressed when the phone rang. He picked up. It was Joe Lawless.

Lawless explained that Bledsoe was in a dither about Dart Man. Or, more to the point, in a dither about the problems Dart Man was causing him downtown.

"He said he wants one of my top investigators on it, and I thought of you," Lawless said, "but if you don't want it, I'll understand."

Benton would say yes to Lawless on just about anything. In his darkest days, when he needed support and love and encouragement, when he needed somebody to say that he was not a piece of crap, it had been Joe Lawless who held out a hand.

"That'll be fine, Joe. Just tell me where and when."

"Well," Lawless said, "at least it will be a break from homicide. How many do you have on the plate now."

"A dozen," Benton said. "It's been slow."

Lawless chuckled.

"Well, why don't you give Dart Man a week or two, and then we'll get you back in squad work."

"Whatever," Benton said.

"Thanks, George," Lawless said.

"Thank you," Benton said.

After he hung up, he reflected on the Dart Man case. He was aware of it, and it was baloney. Benton was something of a medical expert—a confirmed hypochondriac currently in recovery—and he knew, like Bledsoe, that the chance of a woman getting AIDS from a sewing needle was very slim. And, what was more, the tests done on the needles were all negative for any contamination. Why would he start contaminating them?

George left the apartment at around three o'clock. He felt good. George was a young-looking forty-five, and when he dressed the way he normally dressed, which meant expensive, impeccably coordinated clothing, he looked—because he was also a trim, darkly handsome man who resembled the actor Tyrone Power—like a model.

But today he was dressed in suit, sport jacket, and sport shirt. The clothing was still good quality, and well-tailored, but it was not compulsive. He had succeeded in fighting down the urge to look perfect—to look perfect outside because he felt so imperfect inside.

It was a great feeling to let himself be imperfect.

CHAPTER 4

Leo Weissberg had been warned by his three children to get out of the Bronx, to close his jewelry store at 1234 Burnside Avenue. One of his sons, who was a lawyer and who frequently handled cases that took him to Bronx County Courthouse, was particularly concerned. One day he had explained why to his father in no uncertain terms.

"Pop," he had said, "I work the courts and I know what kind of people you have in the Bronx. Not people, animals. These guys will kill you for a nickel bag of crack. They're crazy. And they're getting younger and crazier every day. Do you know how many stores in this area have been burglarized?"

"More than a few," his father said. "I know the dangers. I know a lot about danger and animals."

His son certainly couldn't deny that. At the age of nine Leo had been sent to Dachau, and when he had miraculously emerged at the age of thirteen, his parents and many of the relatives who had gone into the camp with him were no longer alive. Yes, he had known about life and death and animals and man's inhumanity to man for a long time.

His son said the entire family was concerned about him, and begged him to give up the store, but Leo was adamant, too. He would not. Most of his business now was young, Hispanic, and black, and when you got close to these people, you realized that they were like anyone else—people with hopes and dreams, and made of flesh and blood. Leo, who was a merchant as well as a skilled jeweler, provided a product and a service, and he enjoyed his work. He was not about to be scared out.

But he was not a fool. He did not stay open during the evening hours. He was only open when there were people on the street, and he helped the cops out more than a little—they would cruise by every now and then and keep an eye on the place.

Also, when he left the store, he pulled down a corrugated steel door and the plate-glass windows were magnetically taped and tied into a closed circuit alarm system linked to the NYPD.

There was no skylight in the store. To get in, burglars would have to drill through a two-foot-thick ceiling. Leo commented to one of his sons, who did not laugh, that if they were able to get through the ceiling, he should be there to greet them and hand over the store.

The only thing Leo didn't have was a gun. He figured he was too old to use it, and it might cause him more grief than it was worth. If life had taught him one thing—and in fact it had taught him many things—it was that if you live by the gun, you may die by the gun.

On Thursday, Leo Weissberg closed the store at six P.M., the usual time, activating the alarm before he locked the front door, and pulling down the corrugated metal door. He immediately went to his car, an old black Impala, and was on his way to his home in Queens within a minute.

Unknown to Leo, he was being watched.

CHAPTER 5

An hour later Slim Roberts pulled up and parked his Ford Econo van on Burnside Avenue, facing west and some fifty yards beyond the entrance to L&B Jewelers, Leo Weissberg's store. He was facing west, Jerome Avenue behind him. He checked his seat belt. It was tight.

Slim was appropriately named. He was a thin man in his mid-twenties. His arms were heavily tattooed, and he was dressed like a biker. His hair was stringy and brown.

Two men sat in the back of the van, seat belts also on. One, whose name was Angelo Gazza, was short and muscular and dark. The other man, Peter Lumaghi, whose nickname was Rocky, was also dressed more or less like a biker.

All the men wore heavy leather work gloves and had construction hats on. Rocky held a small sledgehammer called a lump hammer, and there were two yellow plastic buckets. Near each man was a Disney character mask.

All three men were armed with 9mm Glock automatics.

Directly behind them, only twenty-five yards from the store, also facing west, was a red Chevrolet Monte Carlo, stolen in Staten Island over the weekend and souped up by Anthony Gazza, who was in the driver's seat. Next to him was also a Disney character mask—Mickey Mouse. He also had an Uzi.

Slim's eyes were on the horizon, where yet another vehicle, this one a gray Toyota, was parked on Burnside facing east, toward Jerome Avenue. In this car, also stolen over the weekend, was Jeff Siegel, watching for cops who might be turning onto Burnside. If the operation was in progress, his assignment was to suddenly pull out and have a fender bender with the cops, delaying and distracting them from the action down the street. He was only to leave once the job was done.

Five minutes after Slim and the two men in back pulled up, they saw the signal. A quick flash of Jeff's lights. No cops were in sight. They all checked their watches. Time.

Slim, who had the motor running, flipped the cigarette he was smoking out the window and glanced in the sideview mirror. Traffic was relatively light and nothing was parked in front of L&B—thanks to the orange safety cone Slim had placed on the street a little earlier.

Slim put the van in reverse and then put the hammer to the floor, taking it from zero to thirty in a few seconds; then he turned the wheel hard and the van jumped the sidewalk curb and smashed into the corrugated door on L&B at thirty-seven miles an hour. The door and the plate-glass window crumbled.

The van stopped, half in and half out of the store. The alarm was clanging like crazy, and passersby were stunned, not knowing what happened. The back doors of the van opened and Rocky and Angelo were out, and then Slim was too. They were all wearing their Disney masks—Pluto, Minnie Mouse, and Donald Duck.

In the store, Rocky used the lump hammer expertly, walking along, smashing the glass cases as he did, Slim and Angelo using the buckets to scoop up the diamonds and assorted jewelry.

Within one minute they had taken everything they wanted and got back into the van and out the front door.

Anthony Gazza was waiting with the souped-up Monte Carlo. Even if a cop car appeared right now, he thought, there was no way they could catch him.

People in the street were still frozen, too shocked to react. All most did was watch, but a few got the idea and exited the scene quickly.

The men piled into the car and then it was gone. They stripped off their masks as they went.

Anthony kept the car at a legal speed, and when they hit the Concourse, they just made the green, making a right turn off it, tooling up the service road, then hitting the main road. They made a left off the main road at 176th Street, and then went down two blocks and hung a right at Clay Avenue.

The gray Toyota was waiting with Jeff behind the wheel.

Anthony pulled the Monte Carlo behind the car and all three men exited, taking everything with them, including the keys, and got into the Toyota. Jeff pulled away.

In the distance they heard the sound of sirens. No one said anything until a couple of minutes later, when they were tooling toward the Major Deegan, on their way back to Brooklyn.

Then Anthony checked his digital watch. A little smile played around his mouth.

"Eight minutes," he said. "Nice. Very nice. Congratulations, gentlemen."

Everyone smiled and shook hands.

CHAPTER 6

In a precinct known for unusual police officers, none were more unusual than Howie Stein and Frank Piccolo, detectives and partners in Joe Lawless's Felony Squad.

First, their appearance was unusual, and in marked contrast to each other. Piccolo was a small, dark-haired man with penetrating dark eyes and a Roman nose. Howie Stein was perhaps three-quarters of a head taller, built bulkily, with a shock of carrot-colored hair and a body covered with freckles. But what made him particularly unusual-looking was his left arm. Like Rod Laver, the Aussie tennis champ of the sixties, Howie's left arm, thanks to years of pulling on dumbwaiters when his father was super of a Bronx building, had developed to almost twice the size of the right. The left was thick and veined and hairy and muscular in the extreme; the right was human-looking.

Piccolo and Stein had similar histories. Each had become known as people to avoid fighting with. The word on Piccolo was that, though small, he was "two quarts low"; a schoolyard fight with him could turn into a fight to the death.

Howie's one-punch knockouts in the schoolyard gave him the nickname of "Thunderfist." It was rumored that he had once coldcocked a steer, though this was not proved.

On the street they had the nickname "Frankenstein," after Frank and Stein, but the name stuck because of the way they conducted business, which was any way they could.

It was Frankenstein who caught what the media called the "crash and dash" squeal. It would be, they thought, a nice change from drug-related killings, which were ninety-nine percent of the homicides in the precinct, and to Frankenstein, boring in the extreme.

Frankenstein did not officially take over the case until the afternoon of the day after it occurred, because both were in court testifying against a very nasty black guy who had killed the owner of a bodega on Tremont Avenue during a heist. Frankenstein had softened him up for testifying by taking him out to Rodman's Neck in the Bronx, making him climb into an empty oil tank, and then bombarding the tank with big rocks for fifteen minutes. When the suspect emerged, he was ready to confess to whatever they wished, including that the moon was made of green cheese.

When they arrived at the crime scene, tape was up and two patrolmen stood guard. In this neighborhood looting was not only expected, but required. No self-respecting denizen of Fort Siberia could pass an open jewelry store without taking something.

Inside, Frankenstein found the crime scene unit working the scene, taking prints, looking for evidence. A white-haired old man was present. He looked to be the owner, pissed and sad at the same time.

Frankenstein went up to him and introduced themselves.

"I'm Frank Piccolo, and this is my partner Howie Stein. You the owner?"

"Yes," the man said, "I'm Leo Weissberg."

"Sorry about the store," Howie said.

Weissberg nodded.

"Are you okay," Piccolo asked, "to answer a few questions?"

"Sure will. Sons of bitches!"

Frankenstein nodded. That was true.

"How much was taken?" Piccolo asked.

"Two hundred thousand, maybe. But I had a number of engraved pieces that are irreplaceable."

"Mr. Weissberg," Stein asked, "did you notice anyone different coming in here over the last few weeks? I mean, someone who might be watching the place? Casing it?"

"I have my regular customers," Weissberg said, "but we also get a lot of new people all the time. I don't know."

"Do you have any employees?" Piccolo asked.

"No. I'm the only one. I don't need anyone else. In the old days we used to have a lot of people. But not anymore," Weissberg said wistfully.

"Excuse us for a moment," Piccolo said. He and Stein walked the length of the store; the floor was littered with glass, and most—but not all—of the velvet-covered trays were empty. One tray had a number of pearl necklaces on it.

They went back to Weissberg.

"Excuse me, Mr. Weissberg," Stein said, "do you know why the robbers left these pearls behind?"

"They know pearls," Weissberg said. "These are just

pretty good copies. Anyone who knows anything could tell the difference between these and the real thing right away."

If there had been a scintilla of doubt in Frankenstein's minds that they were dealing with pros, it evaporated.

They excused themselves again and walked toward the back of the store. There was a crime scene guy working there on a case—or what was left of it. He was young, dark-haired, bookish-looking.

"Anything?" Piccolo asked.

"We've got prints, but who knows who they belong to?"

Frankenstein nodded. They then proceeded into the back room of the store. It was a small, carpeted office dominated almost comically by a huge safe that looked like you'd need an atomic device to open it.

When they went back to the front, the owner was still there, looking around. He could not do anything until the crime scene people said okay.

"Anything taken from the back room?" Piccolo asked.

"No."

"Well, we'd like a list of what you lost, including descriptions."

"I have pictures."

"Good," Stein said.

"I hope you catch them," Weissberg said. "They belong in jail."

"What are you going to do," Stein said, "stay—or move?"

A little fire showed in Weissberg's eyes.

"No way will I move. I'm going to reopen."

"Good," Stein said, and Piccolo nodded.

Outside, there were still a few curious onlookers, and one young black guy with that certain red-eyed look that said crack. Piccolo thought, wouldn't he like to get hold of a couple of pieces of jewelry and hock them for fifty bucks or so?

"I'll take this side," Howie said to Piccolo, meaning he would canvass the stores on his side of the block. Piccolo nodded.

They started to canvass.

It took an hour—about half the stores were closed. Three of the witnesses who saw something were store owners on Howie's side of the street, and two were store owners on Piccolo's side. They had seen practically the whole thing, and were able to describe the bad guys—to a degree.

"They were wearing masks," one said, "of cartoon characters. It was funny and crazy at the same time."

Also, the witnesses said it was obvious that they were young men—the hair that could be seen was not gray, and they moved like young men.

Later, Frankenstein stood on the street and discussed it.

"They sound," Piccolo said, "like a bunch of cocksuckers."

"Young guys."

"There's one gang like this that operates in Manhattan and Brooklyn, I think," Stein said. "Maybe it's them."

"Why the fuck would they come into the Bronx?" Piccolo asked.

Stein shook his head. He had no idea.

Piccolo was about to say something when Leo Weissberg came up to them.

"I was searching my mind," Weissberg said, "and I do remember someone who seemed . . . unusual."

Frankenstein looked at him.

"He came in three or four times over the last month . . . but it was always near the end of the day—just before I closed."

"Did he buy anything?" Piccolo asked.

"Yes, he did buy something. A little pendant—I think on his last trip."

"Didn't you wonder," Piccolo asked, "why he kept coming in and not buying anything?"

"No, people often come back. He said he wanted to buy a ring for his fiancée. This is a major purchase. I never push people."

"Pay by check?" Stein asked.

Weissberg had a pained expression on his face.

"Unfortunately, except in a very few rare instances, I don't accept checks. This is a very bad neighborhood."

"What do you remember about him?" Stein asked.

"Just that he was young. And he had beautiful wavy black hair."

"Long?" Piccolo said.

"No, not really. Just thick and wavy. Nice-looking, too."

"Do you think," Piccolo said, "you could come down to headquarters so we could get a drawing done of this guy?"

"Why not?"

"Good, we can make an appointment."

Or, Stein thought, maybe we'll have a picture to show you already.

CHAPTER 7

When they got back to the Five Three squad room, Piccolo made some calls and found out how many precincts were involved in investigating cases involving a crash-and-dash type gang. Over the last year there had been thirty crash-and-dash assaults on a wide variety of stores: jewelry, fur, and, in two cases, pawnshops. All were places where there was valuable merchandise that could be grabbed quickly. The jobs had been in six different precincts in Manhattan, Brooklyn, and Queens.

Frankenstein was lucky enough to speak with a Sergeant Tommy Kenney in Midtown South. He had been pursuing a gang for quite a while—four *years*.

Kenney's first statement surprised Piccolo.

"We know who's doing it," he said, "but catching them is something else."

"Who?" Piccolo said.

"The Gazza brothers."

"Who are they?"

"Tell you what," Kenney said, "if you want to pop down here when you get a chance, I'll be happy to fill you in on what I know."

"That would be nice," Piccolo said. "When would be good for you?"

"How about now?"

"You got it."

An hour later Frankenstein met Kenney in Sweeney's, an old-fashioned bar at 43rd Street and Eighth Avenue and a favorite watering hole of cops. They took a booth in the back, a couple of empty booths away from the nearest occupied one.

A waitress came by and took their orders, and Piccolo asked the question that had been burning in his mind.

After the waitress departed Kenney took some eight-by-ten color photos out of an envelope. He laid them on the table, side by side. There were five in all, and all surveillance shots. There wasn't a B shot among them.

"Who's this?" Piccolo asked, pointing to a very handsome guy with thick, wavy black hair.

"That's Anthony Gazza, the leader."

"Why haven't you been able to collar them?"

"For one thing, people are afraid of them. They're not known as killers, but they have killed. They can be bad people. Another thing," Kenney said, "is that they're very smart. They know all about wires and pen registers and everything else. Very difficult to get them with their pants down."

Kenney paused, then continued.

"They're just very careful. Anthony Gazza is the younger of the two brothers, but he fancies himself

Rommel in the desert wars. He's a military history nut, and he tries to run his five-man squad like a military organization. He's very big on planning—and planning to cover his ass."

"All-male gang?" Stein asked.

"Yeah. Neither of the Gazza brothers have wives, but they do have girlfriends."

"Maybe we could work one of them, get them to wear a wire."

"I doubt it," Kenney said. "I don't think they'd talk about anything in front of their girlfriends."

"You haven't made any progress at all?" Piccolo said.

"The most progress we made was a former gang member who flipped over."

"What happened?" Stein asked.

"Disappeared."

The men were silent when the waitress came and set down their drinks. Kenney had gathered up the photos before she arrived. They continued when she left.

"These guys are making a lot of money," Piccolo said. "All the capers they pulled, they got to be very smart."

"That's it."

"Are they," Stein asked, "connected?" He meant are they affiliated with a Mafia family.

"No," Kenney said.

"I'm surprised nobody horned in."

"Maybe the Mafia's getting mellow," Kenney said. "Compared to the Colombians or the posses, they look like choirboys."

"Well," Piccolo finally said, "if we could see the files on them, maybe we could find an approach."

"No problem," Kenney said, "you can pick it up any time you want. Just give me enough time to make copies. It's thick."

"I can see why," Stein said.

"One other thing," Kenney said, "if you do find an approach, maybe you could give me and my squad a little piece of it."

"Sure," Piccolo said, and he meant it. You never got anywhere in the cops and robbers world if you were a pig.

CHAPTER 8

Two days following their visit with Kenney, Frankenstein sat at the kitchen table of their third-floor apartment on 204th Street and Bainbridge Avenue in the Bronx. The building was close to, but not actually in, Fort Siberia, which was separated from them by Mosholu Parkway. Piccolo had been heard to say that he would never live in Fort Siberia. "Too dangerous."

It was only nine in the morning. The day promised to be hot, but it was still cool, with a cool breeze coming in the windows, which were open. From the living room, where Piccolo kept his five pets—python, monitor lizard, boa constrictor, tokay gekko, and the centerpiece of his collection, a fully grown wolverine—there was a gentle stirring. Home sweet home.

Piccolo was drinking guinea red, Stein San Pellegrino.

For Piccolo, it was the best of times. Stein and he had been partners and roommates now for three years, and though he still sometimes worried about losing him—his first partner had been gunned down by a posse drug dealer—his concern was not anywhere near as constant as when he first hooked up with him.

Both men were "between spouses"—Piccolo had been divorced a long time, and Stein's had recently come through—but they had each other; and a cop partner relationship, which has the survival instinct as its base, is as close as any human relationship can be.

During the night, they had caught another of the some seventy homicides a year that Siberia always racked up. Surprisingly, this one wasn't drug-related, but was the outcome of two black guys playing a basketball game. One had supposedly "dis'd"—disrespected—the other, so instead of a fistfight, which was the way they might have handled things when Stein and Piccolo were young, the dis'd one had gone home and returned with his 9mm.

"These fucking people," Piccolo said, sipping the wine. "They're worse than wops."

Stein laughed. He had a cackling laugh which, when he was having trouble at the 62nd precinct before being shipped to Siberia, had been recorded by his commanding officer in an attempt to indicate to a deputy chief what kind of maniac he was.

The day before they had gotten the crash-and-dash

case file from Tommy Kenney, and after poring through it thoroughly, they saw no easy way to get at these guys. No grounder, it.

They had established one thing: it was the Gazza brothers they were after. They had showed the pictures of the gang to the jewelry store owner, Weissberg, and he had almost had a shit fit. Yes, Gazza definitely was the man who came into his shop three or four times.

Frankenstein had also showed Gazza's pictures to other people on Burnside. One store owner had seen him.

Stein sipped his Pellegrino.

"A wire is probably out of the picture, if we can believe what Kenney said," Piccolo said.

"I think the very fact that they haven't collared any of the gang proves it won't work," Stein said. "They probably have sweep equipment—the whole nine yards."

Piccolo sipped his wine and lit a cigarette. In deference to Stein, who did not like smoking, Piccolo blew the smoke out the open window as much as possible.

"Maybe," he said, showing a gap-toothed smile—he kept his bridge off around the house, and sometimes on the street—"maybe we should go and pull their hair."

Stein laughed. Three months earlier, brutality charges had almost been filed against Piccolo by a twenty-three-year-old Hispanic male suspected of child abuse. The specific charge stated that during an interrogation, the "victim" had had his pubic hair yanked "violently" by Frank Piccolo, who was "seeking answers to certain unspecified questions." The hair had been actually pulled out of the pubic area, a painful experience.

But the charges were never filed by the victim, Pablo Hernandez, due to a late night meeting with Frankenstein, the content of which they didn't talk about. When cops did things that were way outside the law, they hardly ever talked about them.

"These guys don't sound like the type to wilt under fire," Stein said.

"I was just kidding, really," Piccolo said. "We're going to have to be creative."

"What do you mean, plant something on them?"

"No. Just work hard."

There was silence.

"It would be good if we could find a weak link," Stein said.

Piccolo took a deep drag on his cigarette and blew the smoke out the window.

"According to Kenney, there is no weak link."

"There's got to be some way in."

They were silent for a moment.

"If we could find the fences," Stein said, "we might get to them."

"Flip one of them."

"Yeah," Piccolo said, "use a little friendly persuasion . . ."

"Up to and including," Stein said, "going into body cavities without authorization or anesthesia."

Now Piccolo laughed, and he sounded out to lunch. Stein cackled. The two together sounded like a ward in Mid Hudson Psychiatric Facility.

Piccolo mashed the cigarette out in an ashtray on the kitchen table.

"This is when I miss the Ferret," he said, referring to a four-star snitch who had been caught and whacked by a fat mafioso in Philly.

"Yeah, if anyone could find out who was getting the swag, it would be him."

"Arnie is very good," Stein said, referring to Arnie Shapiro, a pigeon of Stein's who was pretty reliable and had a quality all good snitches needed—large balls.

"All we can do," Piccolo said, "is put out the word through him and some other pigeons. If they can come up with a fence, we'll take it from there."

"You got it."

Piccolo stood up.

"Where you going?" Stein asked.

"To feed Spot." Spot was the wolverine, pound for pound the most vicious animal in the world, a creature so savage that it could drive a bear—which outweighed it ten to one—off its kill.

"I don't think we have anything in," Stein said.

"I'll feed it Johnny Wadd," Piccolo said, referring to the fourteen foot python, and let loose with one of his high cackles. He was soon joined by Stein. It was bedlam again on Bainbridge Avenue.

CHAPTER 9

The Dart Man task force convened in one of the subterranean rooms in the immense rust-colored building that was Police Headquarters in downtown New York City.

The task force consisted of six detectives, each representing a precinct where Dart Man had struck.

Lieutenant Jim Frey, a heavyset, ruddy-faced homicide cop in his early fifties, was in charge of the task force; he also would handle most communication with the media.

Frey was a personable man, a graduate of John Jay College of Criminal Justice and a more than occasional lecturer there. He knew how to steer clear of mine fields, and he could think on his feet. He had a nonadversarial style and was able to take on the most aggressive, swinish reporter and keep his cool.

The rest of the communication duties fell to Colleen McKay, an attractive woman in her mid-thirties who was a deputy chief and head of PR. She would normally help the PC in his press conferences.

Though he was a politician, Frey couldn't bear to bullshit the troops. All of them knew that the case was unimportant except in terms of adverse exposure of the brass by the media. Hence, when he talked to them the first time, his tone was sardonic. He thanked them for taking time out "from your minor concerns such as child abuse, murder, and rape to work this case."

It got a good laugh.

But that was about it for the humor. Cops are part of a military organization—that's why they call civilians civilians—and these cops had been ordered to track Dart Man down, which they would try to do, and as quickly as possible.

The detectives were to be given the full cooperation of the department, and the first step was to refine the composite drawing they had of Dart Man.

"Let's show all the victims the composite," Frey said, "and see if they can add any details that will make it an even closer likeness. Once we do, we'll wallpaper the city with it.

"And while you're at it," he told the assemblage, "let's reinterview them. You guys are supposed to be some of the best interrogators in the department. Maybe the first detectives missed something. This isn't 'Hawaii Five-O.' "

All told, Dart Man had attacked thirty women over a period of three months. They divided the victims equally among the detectives, each drawing five.

For a while Frey and the detectives also concentrated on a city map that showed the locations where Dart Man had struck, in the hope that they could find a pattern; the locations, of course, were marked with—what else—pins.

There was a cluster of attacks in Manhattan, but also single ones in the wilds of Brooklyn and Queens. The map showed little except that the guy was a roving character. He got around.

It was also noted that all the attacks occurred either before ten A.M. or after six P.M. That might indicate that Dart Man held a regular job. There were no attacks on weekends.

Frey also gave a couple of slide presentations.

One showed close-ups of the darts used. There wasn't much there. Thin strips of notebook paper had been fashioned into feathers and glued to very ordinary—and very untraceable—sewing needles.

From the diameter of the dart it was determined that a large, sturdy straw—a couple of the victims had seen the "dart gun"—such as those used at McDonald's, was the gun used.

The task force also tried to profile the victims. Frey showed pictures of some of the women—some would not allow their pictures to be taken. Some were pretty, some not, some black, some Hispanic, some white. All had dark hair, dark eyes, and good figures featuring accentuated, prominent behinds.

"All of these women," Benton volunteered, "have Caledonian rather than callipygian behinds."

He went on to explain that a callipygian behind was a well-formed, solid behind, but not particularly accentuated. "A Caledonian derriere," Benton continued, "is accentuated. In some women its shape is such that you could actually place an object on top of it and it wouldn't fall off."

Some discussion on the subject led the detectives exactly nowhere.

Frey also showed whatever slides had been taken in emergency rooms of the wound areas of naked buttocks. Trying to keep a straight face, he noted that in "seventeen of the cases, the left buttock had been hit, and in thirteen the right."

One of the detectives got a big laugh when he asked if he could take the slides home with him.

Frey sensed after perhaps an hour that the troops were getting bored, and he dismissed them. He suggested they get together every three days. It was all so silly . . . but not to the people who paid their salaries.

Two hours after the meeting, the PC and the mayor, along with Colleen McKay and a couple of chiefs, announced the formation of the task force, which included some of the city's top detectives.

Everybody seemed happy, including the media. The PC had, after all, given them another tool to terrorize the public—and sell papers.

After the meeting, George Benton immediately went about the task of contacting the victims. It was a small-potatoes case, but it did interest him. Just why would a man go around the city shooting needles into women's behinds? To that question, he would definitely like an answer.

CHAPTER 10

The TV stations all picked up the PC's news conference. It was, as they say, good copy, and the newspeople were happy to imply in their presentations that Dart Man held a lot of women hostage to fear, something they reinforced by intercutting interviews with women who were afraid. Of course, there had been a number of women who thought it ridiculous, but they never made it on the tube.

The small black man was in his room at six o'clock when the news came on. He basked in the glory of TV news. It made him feel important and dangerous, a man to be reckoned with.

As he watched, his small eyes slid from the Police Commissioner—and his mind wandered from what he was saying, though he couldn't concentrate well anyway—to the woman standing next to the commissioner.

She was pretty, with dark hair and eyes, and for a moment he didn't know who she was.

And then he remembered. She was the news lady of the police department. Anytime they had a bad thing happen, she would come out and tell everybody to calm down.

The words and the sounds of the commissioner and the reporters asking questions gradually faded, and the man kept looking at the woman. Soon, there was just him and her. It was as if they were in a bubble through which sound couldn't penetrate.

She had, he saw, small breasts, but that was all he could see. He hoped he would get to see more, and then he did. At one point the commissioner turned, walked over to a map and pointed to something on it. As he did, the camera pulled back and caught the woman's legs and ass. They shocked him. Her legs and her sharply curved ass laughed at him, made him feel small . . . and at the same time aroused him.

Then, with the arousal, came the anger. He was very, very angry. It was almost as if the anger were pouring off him like heat. He wanted to drive something into her.

He went to his phone. Actually, it wasn't his phone. It was Aunt Martha's.

He got the number of the police department. It took him a couple of calls, but he got the name of the bitch on TV: Colleen McKay. She was Deputy Commissioner of Public Affairs. Now he had to find her.

Then he blinked slowly, almost like a lizard. His hand touched his erect member.

CHAPTER 11

Benton didn't know it, but the woman who opened the door to the apartment at around three on Friday afternoon was a far cry from the Linda Wolosky who left her apartment Monday morning to go to work.

Different people react to different things in different ways, and Linda had spent some very upsetting nights. In some ways, perhaps, Dart Man's needle had punctured some illusions for her. Just because she was young and pretty and had a good job and a loving boyfriend, she was not invulnerable. Dart Man had shown that she was like everyone else, very vulnerable indeed.

The experience had also made her a little paranoid. On Wednesday she and her roommates had the superintendent install a new dead-bolt lock on the door. And it took a good minute, after double-checking that Benton was who he said he was, before she would open the door.

She had little or no makeup on, and her dark hair was pulled back. Her eyes, which were large and dark, were noticeably bloodshot. She was dressed in a plain dress and slippers.

They went into the kitchen.

"Would you like coffee or something?" she asked Benton.

"That would be good," he said.

As she prepared the coffee at a pantry shelf that lined one wall of the kitchen, he asked her some innocuous questions about where she worked, what she did, and how she liked her job. Finally, when she sat down with the coffee brewing, he got to the meat of it.

"Forgive me," he said, and he meant it, "for having to drag you through this again, but the questions are necessary."

Linda nodded.

"Did you see the man who did this to you?"

"No, I didn't."

"When you were walking to the subway, did you notice anyone following you?"

"Not really."

"You went to the subway alone?"

"Yes."

Benton nodded.

"You know there have been thirty attacks, counting yours. A number of the victims reported seeing a small black man in the area. Anyone like that around?"

"Not that I saw. I mean, Fordham Road has a lot of black people walking on it, especially at that time of day. I was going to work and all."

Benton nodded. The coffee maker had stopped. Linda went over and poured two cups.

"How do you take it?"

"Black," he said, and was not going to say anything else, then did, "with Sweet 'N Low, if you have it."

"Sure. One or two?"

"One," he said, and felt good. It was a small thing,

but progress for him. He always had difficulty expressing his needs.

Linda served the coffee and sat down.

"Have you seen a doctor?" Benton asked.

"Not really," Linda said. "It was nothing."

They paused.

"Did they get the result back on the needle yet?" she asked. "I mean whether it was—"

"No," Benton said, "but I wouldn't worry about it. The media plays it up, but there's little if any chance the needle is contaminated. More than this, there's the pattern of Dart Man. If he were a killer, we would have known it by now."

She looked relieved.

Benton could not think of anything to say. He chewed the fat with her a little longer, and then got up to leave. He went to the door, Linda showing the way.

He turned to say good-bye. She seemed preoccupied.

"You know," she said, "I just remembered one unusual thing, and I don't even know if . . . this man was . . ."

"What's that?"

"A smell. While I was standing on the platform, I smelled something very sweet, like flowers. In fact I thought someone was near me with flowers. But I didn't see any."

"Maybe it was perfume."

"Maybe," Linda said. "But it was powerful. Like someone had used too much. Maybe it was coming from him."

Benton nodded. He thanked Linda Wolosky and was gone.

CHAPTER 12

Colleen McKay, Deputy Commissioner of Public Affairs, had a pretty long and hard day. In fact, it had started at eight o'clock in the morning. When she finally left her office, it was close to ten in the evening.

She walked to the end of the corridor and pushed the button on the elevator that would take her to the garage.

The day had started with the usual press briefings and approval of various releases that would keep a steady flow of information to the media. She wasn't able to breathe before eleven o'clock, and then she processed a wide variety of requests for information on articles and books, guided tours, interviews with various and sundry cops, requests for her to speak, and a hundred other things.

She had no illusions about the job. When she took it, she expected it to be difficult.

For one thing, it was a job that entailed her being chief press officer for the largest and perhaps most active police force in the world. When Colleen had come on the job three years earlier, there had been 26,000 people on the force. Now there were 28,000, and though no one admitted it, the quality was much lower. Indeed, one chief who had recently retired—in disgust—said that in his day they wouldn't let you on the job if they caught you spitting on the sidewalk. Today, they were letting people on the job who had drug records.

The elevator came to her floor and opened. It was empty. She stepped on. It started to descend.

It was, Colleen thought, like a formula. Fewer quality cops led to more problems for her. When a cop was discovered as being dirty, the media loved it, and the phones in her office would go off the hook.

Aside from the increase in problems among cops, there was the invisible wall that had been set up between the old guard and the new, and she was always being tested for her loyalty.

A year earlier, after a search, the black mayor had hired a new PC, formerly a PC in Austin, Texas. The old guard, mostly tough, overweight Irish guys with white hair and ruddy complexions, chafed under this appointment—the Police Commissioner of New York City was supposed to be an Irishman, not a black man.

As one borough chief said in his thick brogue, "You don't appoint blacks, you arrest them."

But the fundamental division was not racism; it was favoritism. The new commissioner had established that if you were black, you had it made; if you were white, you might as well have been black—under a white Irish PC.

Also, there was the fact that Colleen was female, and not a cop. Contrary to what anyone said, she knew that most cops were chauvinists and resented her presence, though more than a few respected her.

But it was that final gulf that she couldn't cross, that no one could cross unless they were a cop. Cops treated other cops differently than they treated civilians.

All this notwithstanding, she loved the job. She had grown tremendously in it—a Colorado River of problems did that to you, and she was very happy she had taken it.

She worked, of course, directly for the PC, and she was white, but she could live with his racism, if that's what it was. Weren't most people a little racist? It was just part of being human. In many other ways, the new PC was a good cop and a good person.

The doors opened on the garage, which always had uniformed security personnel around. The official vehicles of the top officials in the department were parked here, and no one wanted anyone who was unauthorized in the garage, wiring a bomb to the manifold of the PC's car.

She waved to one of the uniformed people as she approached her car.

"How are you, Commissioner?"

"Not bad," she said, "still less than half a day."

The uniformed cop laughed.

She got into a black Ford sedan, which was a perk of the job, and warmed it up.

She did not feel tired, mentally or physically. She felt good, because she ate well and worked out regularly.

She also knew she looked good. And though it was a form of reverse chauvinism, she knew it didn't hurt to be a good-looking broad working among men.

Colleen only had one little problem that nagged at her. She wanted to get married again. She had been married once, and it hadn't worked out. But she wanted to get married and, in a couple of years, have kids. If she didn't, she had a feeling that she would regret it. Even a superb press release can't hug you.

She exited the garage, driving out onto West Street. It was raining lightly so she turned on her wipers.

She looked uptown. The city was becoming blocks of glass that masqueraded as architecture. She hated it. The city itself had changed, too. It looked more or less the same, but there was anger and hatred now like never before.

She sometimes wondered, sadly, where it would all lead.

Colleen lived in Jamaica Estates, in Queens. Some sections of Queens, such as Jamaica itself, had been infested with crack and its concomitant ills, but not Jamaica Estates. It was essentially as it had always been, miles of quiet, tree-lined streets flanked by artfully manicured and landscaped lawns and greenery on which were set some of the most beautiful homes in the city; Tudor-style brick homes topped with gray slate or orange tiles. The entire area had an almost European flavor.

Colleen lived in a luxury apartment house on 178th Street and Hillside Avenue, a massive cream-colored building featuring an awning, underground garage, and round-the-clock security in the form of individuals who monitored who came into the building via a bevy of black and white TV monitors. What's more, you could not get into the building without being announced, via radio, at the desk.

Gus, the night man, was the best security guy, in Colleen's opinion. He was always alert and very tough. He carefully watched anyone who approached the underground garage, and on two occasions he had raced into the garage to help tenants in trouble with his Louisville Slugger in hand.

Colleen often came home late, and she felt secure with Gus on the desk.

She waved at him as she drove past the front entry, which was flanked by glass and gave Gus a clear view outside. Then she drove slowly down the ramp to the garage, activating the electronic door with her control. The door rattled up.

The garage was empty. She parked in her space, 269, got out of her car and locked the doors behind her.

She headed for a small elevator in the corner of the garage that would take her to the main floor.

Suddenly, she flushed with fear. A small black man had materialized from behind one of the concrete support posts.

She did not recognize him, and she assumed she was in trouble. She did not carry a gun, nor any weapon. She did not know if Gus's TV monitors of the garage could see the section she was walking in.

She decided to gut it out. Her satchel purse was pretty heavy. . . .

And maybe he was harmless, maybe had a good reason for being there. Still, the garage seemed particularly small now. The ceiling was so very low.

He approached her and went right by her. She caught a whiff of body odor and something sweet. . . .

Gooseflesh had bloomed on her neck, and she heard a *pfft!* sound and felt a stinging sensation in her right buttock. She screamed and lashed out at him with her pocketbook, and saw him start to run away.

"Gus! Gus! Gus!"

She ran after him. He made it through a door at the other end of the garage and then he was gone.

A moment too late Gus burst from the elevator with his Louisville Slugger in hand.

"What'sa matter? What's the matter?"

"A man . . . fired a dart at me. . . ."

"Where'd he go?"

She pointed to the door, and Gus ran toward it.

CHAPTER 13

Lee Green, the PC, was angry. Or at least that's the way Kenneth O'Brien, Chief of Command, read him. Green, O'Brien had observed, was a tall, bookish kind of man and a cool customer—which was why he survived in politically charged environments. He kept his feelings, mostly, to himself. You had to very carefully read his face to know what he was feeling.

O'Brien watched his eyes. When they narrowed, as they were now, he was pissed.

Green was behind the desk in his office at One Police Plaza, a room with so many couches that it looked like a furniture store, sitting behind a massive desk once occupied by Teddy Roosevelt himself.

O'Brien, in full uniform, was sitting directly in front of Green. In a chair to O'Brien's left was Nick Bonti, Chief of Detectives, and to his left, Lieutenant Jim Frey, head of the Dart Man task force. On O'Brien's right was Colleen McKay.

"When I call the mayor about this," he said, "I want to be able to brief him completely. I don't have to tell you how embarrassing this is going to be for him . . . and us."

Colleen McKay felt her face flush. How about me, she thought, how embarrassing is it going to be for me? In fact, her original idea had been to keep it quiet. No apparent harm was done. But she knew that was stupid. The New York press was a pit bull terrier, and if they got wind of it, they would be in their righteous, arrogant, self-serving glory.

What they were engaged in now, Colleen thought, was damage control. How to get the message out so it did the minimum amount of damage to the department. How to brief the right people the right way.

Everyone in the room was, to one degree or another, considering some disturbing questions raised by the attack—and some disturbing implications. How did Dart Man find out where Colleen lived? If he could find out where she lived, who else was vulnerable? The wife of the Chief of Detectives, the PC's wife . . . the mayor's wife, God forbid!

The PC raised that very question.

"Have you people given some thought to who might be next? Maybe another official's wife?"

The Chief of Detectives had, and he exercised some damage control of his own.

"Yessir," he said, "that occurred to us right away. But we don't believe it would be a problem unless the person fits the profile."

"Yes sir," Frey chimed in, "the perp only attacks a certain kind of woman. . . ."

Bonti nodded in affirmation.

McKay blinked and felt her face redden. Yeah, ones with nice asses, she thought.

"I think," Frey said, "we all know the profile."

"I know it," the PC said flatly. "My wife fits it."

"Maybe what we should do, sir," O'Brien said, "is increase security in the building until we get this guy."

Green nodded. He looked at Colleen.

"Do you have any idea how he got your address?"

This was one question Colleen didn't want asked. She had thought about it, and the answer was obvious. And in retrospect, stupidly embarrassing.

"I'm in the book," she said, "the Queens phone book."

"Why?" Green said.

"I didn't see anything wrong with it. It's a common name, and I'm in there under C—not Colleen. I think twenty-five McKays are in there."

She knew there were. She had counted them that very morning in preparation for this meeting.

"The bottom line is that I didn't see anything wrong

with it. My position doesn't entail making direct enemies, as yours does, sir."

Green realized that she had a point, and though he was pissed, the best thing would be to drop the anger and try to think clearly. Anger wasn't going to accomplish anything.

"Well, you'll talk to the detectives . . . the one good thing we got out of it is that you can make an eyeball identification of this guy, right?"

"Yes sir."

"The other thing I'm concerned about," Green said, "is just how we're going to present this to the media."

There was silence. Then Colleen spoke. "My inclination was to . . . lie. . . ."

All the people in the room, including the PC, laughed.

"That's not the way to go. Give all the facts. Just hold back what's necessary for the detectives to do their jobs."

The PC nodded.

"Sounds okay to me."

"Fine." Jim Frey said. "When could you talk with us about this guy?"

"As soon as possible," Colleen said. "We'll prepare a release on this, and then take it from there. Okay?"

"Okay."

The PC looked at Ken O'Brien.

"We'll talk again," he said, and the meeting broke up. Everyone in the room had the feeling it was going to get worse before it got better.

CHAPTER 14

Anthony Gazza parked the newly stolen black Monte Carlo on the third-floor level of a multilevel gray concrete municipal parking structure on Jerome Avenue and 190th Street. He had previously given the black guy in the booth a fin to keep an eye on it. This was a neighborhood where, if you wanted to keep your car on the street for more than a few hours, you'd better use a heavy chain to secure the hood, or take the battery with you. But it was even at risk in a garage. Crackheads were not particular.

Anyone who knew anything about cars—and spics knew a lot about cars—would know that the Monte Carlo was a classic. They would take the car off the street real quick. If there were some mules—professional car thieves—in the area, one look at the car would make them buggy and they would grab it right away.

The only place where Anthony left any car—in this case his own beloved 1979 Monte Carlo—was on the street in the section of Brooklyn where he lived with his brother, their current squeezes, and sometimes the crew members.

Everybody knew that the car belonged to Anthony Gazza. Therefore, no one would touch it.

Anthony walked up to Fordham and then headed west.

He had begun looking at stores in the area six months ago—this was his third trip this month alone. Above all, he believed in doing his homework. Did Patton look at a map before he went into Italy? Did Rommel know exactly where the British were? Did Dwight Eisenhower study the weather maps feverishly before D day?

They all did, and Anthony Gazza did. The key to the success of an operation was planning and keeping your enemy guessing.

Gazza was dressed to the nines. He had on a beautiful blue suit worth about $1200, a $75 tie, and $300 Italian shoes. His luxurious, wavy, glossy hair was combed to perfection. He wore an expensive ring on each finger and a Rolex.

This time the target was an Antonovich fur store. Gazza had done seven of them before this. As he wryly remarked to gang members one night, "Brand loyalty is important. We wouldn't want to be disloyal."

The store was on Fordham Road between a corner cigar store and a *cuchifritos* restaurant, and not too far from the Jerome Avenue elevated train station.

Just last week something good had happened, as far as Gazza was concerned. Con Ed started working on Jerome and Fordham, making the road difficult to pass. It would effectively block cops in a panic-style situation. Of course, Fordham Road was always crowded.

A few minutes after he left the garage, Gazza was standing in front of the store. He pressed the buzzer, and a man inside dressed in a dark suit and with longish blond hair and glasses emerged. He was looking over Anthony as he came.

He did not hesitate. He opened the door.

"Yes sir," he said.

"I see you sell furs," Gazza said, "that's why I'm here."

The man, whom Gazza estimated to be about fifty and gay, hesitated a moment, then opened the door wide, and Anthony went by him. Inside, Anthony said:

"I heard that you can get pretty good deals in this outlet, and I'm looking for something for my girlfriend. Maybe a sable or a mink."

"Yes sir," he said, "you came to the right place."

Yes, I did, Anthony thought to himself as he looked around.

CHAPTER 15

Even for Fort Siberia, the homicide squeal that Frankenstein caught was gruesome, and it temporarily diverted attention from the crash-and-dash capers. A young couple living in a shithole of an apartment on 179th Street had killed their colicky five-month-old baby one night and fed the remains to their German shepherd. Then they claimed the dog had attacked it and eaten it, which was disproven in a day.

Even for Frankenstein, who had seen enough in their

years working on the job, particularly in Siberia, to make a stone cry—and retch—this one made them look silently and in awe at just how loathesome and perverse fellow members of their race could be.

They simply locked the couple up, and the dog was turned over to the ASPCA, which said that the best course of action was the one they ultimately took: "euthanize" the dog.

Frankenstein felt disgusted and saddened by the whole thing, and they didn't have any desire to bury the couple. They were just two sick young fucks.

It wasn't until two weeks after the first crash-and-dash job that they got back on the squeal, which meant checking in with their snitches.

Frankenstein had put the word out to five pigeons to try to get a lead on where the Gazzas fenced their swag, but it was highly unlikely that they had come up with anything. The snitches would have called them.

Over the period of two days, they contacted them all. The first four didn't have anything, except reasons why they couldn't get anything.

"Even if someone knows something," said one, "and I doubt that many people know much of anything, they are reluctant to talk. Anybody who knows the Gazza brothers are afraid of them, and Anthony Gazza has let it be known on the street that a flannel mouth will not be tolerated."

Another source confirmed what Frankenstein had suspected—no one knew much of anything.

"You start to really understand," Piccolo said, "why none of the other guys have cleared this fucker. No one will talk, and without that, we're not going to get anywhere, unless we use extraordinary methods."

To Frankenstein, extraordinary methods meant framing the bad guys for crimes they didn't commit so that they would go to jail for crimes they did commit but couldn't get convictions on.

They had only done it a few times, and the crime had to be very serious. Both men were not comfortable with it unless the guys were really bad.

So far, the Gazzas did not qualify for a railroad ride to the pen. Anyway, Frankenstein hadn't exhausted all their investigative tools.

It took them an additional day before they could contact the fifth snitch, Arnie Shapiro, their best guy. Arnie never called them, whether he had something or not. He loved to play games—with himself as the puppeteer.

Arnie was special in Frankenstein's eyes, almost on a par with the legendary August "The Ferret" Rondolpho.

Arnie was a thirty-one-year-old heavyset guy who was always going on diets that didn't work; a career snitch and thief who had balls that were as big as his considerable ass. Frankenstein knew that when Arnie was providing certain select cops with information, he was also shoplifting, robbing cars, and occasionally burglarizing. But he wasn't a heist man or a shooter or into drugs—his only addiction was "chocolate cake"—and they tolerated it all because of the quality of information he could normally supply. If Arnie failed, Frankenstein would have given up the snitch route.

When they called him, Arnie said, "I got some good

stuff for you. Much better than finding out who their fence is."

Frankenstein arranged to meet with Arnie in the Blue Bell Diner in Closter, New Jersey, where Arnie was known but Frankenstein wasn't. Arnie always picked a diner to meet in because he knew that in addition to the gelt that would be forthcoming, Frankenstein would pay for the meal. He always arrived an hour early so that he could be on his third wedge of chocolate cake and thereafter devote himself to the business at hand.

Frankenstein knew exactly what Arnie was doing, but they tolerated it. He was a star.

Frankenstein came into the Blue Bell at two-thirty in the afternoon. Arnie was at a table in the back eating a piece of chocolate cake, with a large glass of milk nearby.

Piccolo looked at Stein.

"He looks like he put on another twenty-five pounds since we last seen him."

Stein shook his head. "More than twenty-five," he said.

They had last seen him six weeks ago.

Arnie, smears of chocolate cake around his mouth, smiled when he saw Frankenstein.

"Frank, Howie, how you doin'?"

"That depends," Piccolo said, "on what you got."

Arnie looked at them. He was balding and had a flattish face, dark eyes, and a heavy five o'clock shadow. "I got something good for you."

Piccolo nodded. Sometimes he and Howie would let Arnie play his little game, build up whatever he had into the importance of the combination to the safe at Fort Knox, but their patience level was low.

"Arnie," Piccolo said, "why don't you cut to the chase?"

"Hey, Frank, no problem," he said, forking the cake into his mouth. "Whatever you want. We are here to serve."

Howie thought that when Arnie spoke of himself as "we," it was the right pronoun to use.

"I couldn't, like I told you on the phone, find out anything about their fence. Nobody knows anything, nobody will talk about anything. They want to stay ambulatory and taking nourishment."

Howie laughed. Piccolo smiled.

"What I did find out," he said, blotting his mouth with a napkin, "is where the Gazzas might do their next job."

He looked coyly at Frankenstein, who were excited. Arnie's information was always a hundred percent.

"Where?"

Arnie glanced around even though there was no one within the diner equivalent of nine miles of them.

"Fordham Road," he said, "your precinct."

"Where?"

"That I don't know."

"That you don't know?" Piccolo said. "Fordham Road is long. Can you narrow it down? That's like telling us that he's going to hit somewhere in Idaho."

"Frank," Arnie said, "no need to be sarcastic. I'll narrow it down."

"I'm sorry," Piccolo said, "I'm a little testy."

57

Arnie nodded.

"Anthony Gazza was spotted last week on Fordham Road near Jerome Avenue by one of my operatives. He was dressed in a nice suit, all dolled up . . . right? I mean," Arnie said, "what the fuck is he doing in the Bronx?"

Frankenstein nodded. Arnie's point was well-taken. He was casing some joint or joints.

"What's over there?" Piccolo asked.

For a moment Arnie didn't answer. He was looking toward the slowly revolving dessert case about ten yards away. He was mesmerized—his eyes flat and glazed—as he fixed on the chocolate cake.

Should he, he thought, have a fourth slice? No. I got to start my diet soon.

"I don't know," Arnie finally answered, "but I think there are a couple of fancy stores over there. I'm sure he's not taking a read on a bodega."

Frankenstein nodded. It was their stomping ground. There was a fur store and at least two jewelry stores—plus a nice men's clothing store.

"Is that it?" Frankenstein said.

"Yeah," Arnie said. "What do you want, the date and time? I'm sure you can take it from here."

Frankenstein nodded. They could.

Piccolo reached into his pocket and withdrew greenbacks which were in a roll with a rubber band around it.

"Is five hundred enough?" Piccolo said, rolling the money toward Arnie, who let it come to a stop against his milk glass. Arnie got a pained expression on his face.

"These are bad people," he said. "I'm taking a big chance."

"There's seven hundred fifty there," Piccolo said, and Arnie smiled. He liked dudes who were fast on their feet, and Frankenstein certainly was.

Frankenstein got back to the precinct about five-thirty. They checked the stores near Fordham. Closest to Jerome was the Antonovich fur store, and not too far from them the two jewelry stores. They would check them all out in the morning.

CHAPTER 16

The next morning, at around nine o'clock, Frankenstein showed a picture of Anthony Gazza to the store owners near where he had been seen.

The jewelry-store owners did not remember anyone who looked like Anthony Gazza.

The owner of the fur store, a blond-haired dude, remembered him well.

"He was very well-groomed, very polite. He seemed very interested in buying one of our more expensive furs. He has been here twice."

"When?"

"A few days ago—and maybe two weeks before that."

"Did he buy anything?" Howie asked.

"No, he didn't. He said that it was a big decision and that he wanted to make sure that he got the right garment for his fiancée. I definitely got the feeling that he was going to be coming back."

Frankenstein was sure, too.

"Is he a criminal?"

"Yes," Piccolo said, "he is."

"What do I do if he comes in again?"

"Nothing. Just treat him like he's a regular customer. And as soon as he leaves," Piccolo said, "give us a ring."

He handed the man, whose name was Foster, a business card.

"Thanks for your help," Howie said as they were leaving.

"You close the regular time today, right?"

"Yes, five o'clock. You know how it is. The predators come out at night."

If the Gazza gang was following its pattern, they would not hit the store until after closing time. Frankenstein had some time to prepare a welcoming committee.

An hour after they had visited the fur store, they were in the office of the CO, Captain Bledsoe. Also in the room was Joe Lawless, a hard-looking man who resembled the late actor Steve McQueen.

Lawless had just explained to Bledsoe how Piccolo and Stein had been able to unearth a good lead on the

Gazzas. Bledsoe had previously been briefed by Lawless about the Gazzas and knew they were hot suspects on the crash-and-dash capers.

"Sir," Lawless said, "Frank and Howie feel that the Gazzas are going to be hitting the Antonovich store soon, and that the best thing we can do is provide surveillance on it, which shouldn't be difficult."

Bledsoe's mind was working overtime. This would be a nice feather in his cap. Those Manhattan hotshots had been working on this case for years, literally, with no results. Once they hit Siberia—bang—his two detectives clear it. But there was a problem.

"The problem is personnel," he said to Lawless. "You know as well as I do that we can't afford many people for very long."

Lawless nodded. As Felony Squad commander with a big backlog of work, he understood exquisitely.

"I did have an idea, sir," he said, "that might work."

Bledsoe looked at him. He didn't like Lawless because he was such a hotshot hardhead, but he would be a jerk not to accept the fact that he was a very good detective.

"What's that?"

"We could bring in some people from other precincts to help us. It would just take a few."

Bledsoe nodded. The one thing he didn't want was for the other people, in case of a bust, to get the credit for this. He wanted that.

"That's okay," Bledsoe said, "but who would be in charge?"

"Frank and Howie. This is their turf, this is their squeal."

"Okay," Bledsoe said, "just as long as we make that very clear."

"No problem," Lawless said. They thanked Bledsoe, who said he would get on it right away—and get back to them within an hour. Frankenstein and Lawless left.

A minute later Bledsoe was waiting on the line for Chief John Slaughter to come to the phone. When he did, Bledsoe brought him up to speed on the crash-and-dash case.

"We want to put the store under surveillance," he said, "but we don't have that many people. So I had this idea," he said, "to use a few people from other precincts who had been involved in the case, much like you guys did on the Dart Man case. Except we'd have responsibility from here."

Bledsoe had almost succeeded in making it sound like Slaughter's idea. He had certainly succeeded in kissing his ass.

There was a silence.

"I like it," Slaughter said. "Do it. Any questions or comments, you have them call me."

"Yes sir."

Bledsoe hung up. Sometimes he thought he was a genius.

Chapter 17

Surveillance of the fur store was not that difficult. Fordham Road was a busy street, and therefore if and when the Gazzas hit the store, they would be less likely to notice any cops. Three two-man teams were watching the store by closing time on the same day Bledsoe spoke with Slaughter.

They took advantage of the Con Ed work on Jerome Avenue. Howie and Piccolo donned yellow work uniforms and sat in the back of a Con Ed van some fifty yards from the storefront.

Another team, this one from the Six Five in Manhattan, was in a specially equipped surveillance van almost directly across the street. It was disguised as a plumbing van. And there were two men, each armed with high-powered rifles, on the department store roof directly across the street from the fur store.

Frankenstein wanted to put another team in the store, but the proprietor was not too thrilled with this idea and they abandoned it.

Everything was in perfect readiness. They only needed the Gazzas to show up that day—or the next. Frankenstein felt sure they were coming, but they hoped it would be soon. They simply couldn't spend a lot of time on a stakeout.

* * *

On the third night, the Gazzas came. But unlike any of the other plans they had worked out, this one was a little different.

The assault started at 6:02.

A plain beige 1978 Cutlass, looking very much like a plainclothes car, wheeled off the Concourse onto Fordham Road. Inside, a red bubble-gum light on the dashboard was on and the siren was hammering. It pulled to a shrieking halt near the subway. Before he got out of the car, the driver shouted into a radio tuned to Channel 9, the police frequency. "Officer needs assistance! Signal ten-thirteen! Ten-thirteen! Officer down! Officer down! Grand Concourse and Fordham Road. Hurry!"

The response of cops to a signal 10-13 was nothing short of frenzied. Within minutes every sector car in the area was barreling toward the Grand Concourse and Fordham Road . . . including the officers staking out the Antonovich store.

Frankenstein were on their way within seconds, and so were the cops in the other van. The two rooftop cops did not have a car, but they hoofed it down the stairs and started racing up Fordham toward the Concourse, rifles at the ready.

Slim pulled onto Fordham from Jerome Avenue at 6:05. In the distance he could hear the sounds of sirens.

His instructions had been to wait until 6:06. He waited.

At 6:06 he swung the van into high gear in reverse and hit the Antonovich window going twenty-five miles per hour. The van stopped—half in and half out of the store. The door opened and out poured Angelo Gazza and Rocky and Slim. This time they had stocking masks on.

They quickly and expertly tore the coats off the rack and stuffed them in plastic bags.

One minute later they were on their way out of the store.

Anthony Gazza was waiting in the black Monte Carlo. They piled in, peeling their masks off when they were a hundred yards from the scene.

He moved briskly across Fordham toward University.

"We were set up," he said. "We picked a good day for a diversion."

In fact, Anthony had no good reason why he had created the diversion. It was just part of being a good commander. It was a very satisfying experience and he felt very proud.

On the Concourse and Fordham it was bedlam.

A gaggle of cops were at the car with the red bubble light, trying to figure out what was going on. Frankenstein ran up.

"There's no cop here," a black uniformed cop said, "and this doesn't look like a standard car. What the fuck is goin' on?"

Just at that moment, far behind them, they heard the sound of a crash.

It took Piccolo four seconds and Stein five seconds to get it.

"Fuck!" Piccolo screamed, startling the black cop.

He and Howie started back toward the store, but they knew they would be too late. And they were right.

CHAPTER 18

All around Fort Siberia, and in the other two precincts that had supplied people for the stakeout, there was wailing. Not only had there been another robbery, but the cops were made to look like dogshit. The whole story found its way to the media the next morning and it stank like diarrhea in front of a fan.

All too soon the call came to Bledsoe that he had been dreading. It was Chief Slaughter.

"Why," Slaughter wanted to know, "wasn't anyone put in the back of the store? Isn't that the normal procedure?"

"The detectives tried to, sir, but the proprietor wouldn't allow it."

"This was pressing police business! He should have been made to."

Bledsoe was going to say "we tried," but he knew Slaughter wouldn't be listening. Slaughter was just chewing ass to cover his own. In fact, Bledsoe had detailed the plan to him. Why the fuck didn't he insist on having a team in the store then?

Slaughter worked Bledsoe over a few more minutes, then finished by saying that any future plan "concocted" to trap the Gazza brothers would have to be carefully examined and cleared by headquarters. It made Bledsoe feel about six years old and scared as hell. He pictured himself being in Fort Siberia forever. He would rather retire and spend his life with his wife.

After he hung up, Bledsoe felt frustrated and wanted to unload his frustration on someone—but he couldn't, not without problems. He would only frustrate himself more if he unloaded on Joe Lawless. Nothing ever bothered Lawless. And Piccolo and Stein? They were nuts. He always felt there was a possibility, if he pushed them, that one of them would draw down on him, or maybe Stein would crush him with that gruesome arm.

It was just going to be another shit sandwich day at Fort Siberia.

Frankenstein were in their apartment in the Bronx. They were sitting at the kitchen table, the usual items in front of them. Piccolo had his jug of guinea red and Stein had his mineral water. It was the morning after the robbery, only a half hour after Slaughter had chewed out Bledsoe.

Piccolo sucked deeply on a cigarette and blew the smoke out the window.

He said, "They must be laughing now, that they fucked us over."

"Probably," Stein said.

Piccolo took a sip of his wine and put the glass on the table.

"So what do you want to do?"

"I don't know."

"We know where they live," Piccolo said, "we could drop a half a kilo on them."

Stein was silent.

"I guess, but that bothers me."

"Why? Why not? They fucked us, we fuck them," Piccolo said. But he knew it wasn't that simple for Howie. Howie was a thinker. He sometimes surprised Piccolo with the stuff he could come up with.

"No," Stein said, "not on philosophical grounds. But it bothers me to do it that way because then they would have beaten us. That bothers me. To take them off the street, we have to play the game by our rules. I'd rather play the game by regular rules—more or less—and get them that way. You know what I mean, Frank?"

"I can dig it," Piccolo said, "but if we play by the rules, we're going to have real problems. Where do we go from here? We're tapped out as far as snitches go, these guys are too slick to be collared through regular investigation . . . I don't know."

Stein nodded. Frank was right. It would be difficult.

He sat there thinking as Piccolo got up and went to take a whiz. Where were the Gazza brothers vulnerable?

He couldn't think of anything. Piccolo returned and sat down.

"Can you think," Stein said, "of any place where they might be soft?"

Piccolo shook his head. "We're dead, right? Without talk, we have nothing."

Stein nodded. They were going around in circles, like Indians around a wagon train. There was no way in.

Then, just like that, the germ of an idea.

"Maybe," he said, "we're not talking to the right people. Maybe somebody else, other than the snitches, could help us."

"Who?"

The idea had more or less formed in Howie's head. He was not that excited about it because he wasn't sure it would work and he didn't know exactly whom they would talk to.

"Well," Howie said, "let me lay it out and then you can tell me if it's worth anything. One thing is for sure, it will take a little time to do—if we can do it, and I just hope that there's not another robbery in the meantime."

Piccolo mashed his cigarette out in an ashtray and lit another.

"Nobody in the gang is vulnerable, right?" Stein began.

"That's a given."

"Okay, we got to put pressure on a fence or someone outside the gang who knows the inner workings."

"Okay. Where do we find that out? Our snitches are no good."

"So, we find out—from *other bad guys*. Nothing happens in this town without some bad guys knowing what their colleagues are doing. At least some bad guys."

"The Mafia?"

Stein pointed a finger at Piccolo. "That's exactly right. The Mafia would know. And who do we know who owes us a little favor?"

69

"Neil Falco," Piccolo said. "And it's more than a little favor."

"That's right," Stein said. "You're right."

And indeed it was more than a little favor. Frankenstein had learned while investigating a Colombian drug scam that Neil Falco, the head of the biggest Mafia family in New York—and therefore America—was scheduled to be whacked. They told him and saved his life.

"I propose talking to him," Stein said.

"Let's see if we can arrange it."

"Good."

"Those Gazzas may be laughing now," Piccolo said, "but in the end they'll be laughing out of their ass."

CHAPTER 19

The media went after Dart Man's attack on Colleen McKay like sharks after chum. They loved it, and a number of jokes started to make the rounds. Colleen heard several which got past her normally tough hide. For a week after the attack, she wore loose-fitting skirts because she started feeling self-conscious, but then decided she couldn't go on like that forever and went back to her regular dress.

The one good thing that resulted from the attack was that she was the first victim to see Dart Man very clearly. She saw him full face on, and despite the fear that she felt as he approached her in the garage, she was able to record his features quite accurately. Two days after the attack, a drawing showing a black man with fairly bushy hair, small dark eyes, and a thin nose was given to the media. In an instant the face of Dart Man was shown in millions of homes.

The publicity brought in hundreds of responses and a concomitant work load for the members of the task force. All of the leads had to be checked out.

Over a seven-day period, George Benton checked out seventy-five separate leads. Some turned out to be well-meaning people thinking they knew who Dart Man was, while others were people trying to shaft ex-husbands or ex-wives or ex-lovers. Some were the handiwork of what cops called "ray people"—folks who said that they got the information on Dart Man from outer space.

Benton was working sixteen-hour days to check out leads, but at the end of ten days the task force was no closer to making a collar and the leads were starting to peter out.

However, there hadn't been another attack.

Benton finally had a little time to spend with Ellen Stevens nearly two weeks after the attack on Colleen McKay. She made a special chicken dish, which he liked, and they enjoyed some white wine. Benton took a sip of the wine and looked across the candlelight at her.

And it was beautiful how he could talk to her. She was no raving beauty, but she had a soft face with nice features and especially beautiful eyes and hair.

"In the past," he said, "I would have felt really bad about not clearing this case. Like it was my fault that this guy was still on the loose. But I don't feel that way now, and you've had a lot to do with that."

Ellen smiled. "I don't think so. I think it's you and your growing realization that you can be worth something even though you're not perfect."

"You mean," Benton said, "no one's perfect?"

"No," Ellen said, "not even Joe Lawless."

"He comes close."

"He probably has a lot of anger in him."

"You only met him once," Benton said.

"That's what I sensed," Ellen said. "I could be wrong."

"Why?"

"Because . . . I'm not perfect."

Benton laughed. "I must say," he said, looking at the table, "I find it hard to believe that you love me. You could have any number of guys."

"Sure," she said, "but not like you. Do you know how many people in this world are sensitive to the needs of others?"

"Well, my view is jaundiced from being a cop. We don't see many sensitive folks."

"There really aren't many," Ellen said, "and when you meet someone who is caring, and also happens to be a very attractive man—that's a potent combo."

"A potent combo—and an impotent man."

"Sometimes," she said, "sometimes not. So what?"

Benton took another sip of wine and felt the urge for

a cigarette. But he had given them up for the hundredth-odd time.

"I get the feeling that you have endless understanding."

"I get mad," Ellen said, "you know that. But . . . it's sad to see people go from the cradle to the grave never knowing what life could be like. They live dreams that never can come true, and nightmares that exist only in their own minds."

Benton thought for a second. He said, "It seems that the real problems people have exist only in their own minds. Life is not that bad. It's how you look at it, and how you look at it is how you react to it and how you live it."

"I think that's well said," Ellen said, "except that all that is conscious is feelings, usually. You have anger, say, you know not where it's from, and you project it onto the world and act on it."

Benton said, "Speaking of anger, what do you think of Dart Man?"

"It's a good segue," Ellen said, "because I think the essence of Dart Man is anger. That's what he's feeling when he fires those darts into women. Rage, anger, hatred."

"Why?"

"It could be any number of reasons," Ellen said, "but you can be sure that the women he attacks are symbols of the person he hates, for whatever reason."

"That's how it was with the serial murderer I went after," Benton said.

"You've never talked about that much."

"It happened a few years ago. When I did a background on the guy—his name was Albert Brooks—I found that all the women he had killed looked like his mother, who had abused him."

"Right," Ellen said, "that's usually the way it works."

"You think this guy will stop? I mean spontaneously. Some serial murderers do."

"I doubt it," Ellen said, "because it fills a need that cannot be satisfied."

"But some serial murderers stop."

She said, "Not because they want to. Maybe their life situation changes and that stops them. Do you think Ted Bundy would kill again if, by some miracle, he suddenly were brought back to life?"

"Sure," Benton said, "he'd kill forever."

"That's what I mean."

"Do you think that the dart is phallic? It would seem to be."

"No question. The sex object is the target of his rage. The dart is the way he savages the sex object. He probably has quite violent masturbatory fantasies."

"Welcome to the club," Benton said.

Ellen laughed, but then she grew serious. "I just hope that it doesn't get worse."

"What do you mean?"

"Whatever. This guy is carrying around a heavy load."

Benton said, "I haven't asked you this, but do you have any idea where we might find him?"

"No," Ellen said, "not really. That's your job, buddy."

Benton nodded.

"You have one other job," Ellen said.

"What's that?"

"Coming around the table and giving me a kiss."

Benton obeyed.

Chapter 20

Dart Man was in his room watching TV. His aunt was at her job as a hospital aide.

He sat in a battered old armchair and watched the television. He was waiting for "A Current Affair" with Maury Povich. He liked that show because the sluts got killed. It was easy to tell who the sluts were. You just had to look at their bodies. If their bodies jutted out behind, that meant that they were showing things. They wanted you to see things. They were dirty sluts and should be punished.

He lit a small cigarillo, inhaled deeply, then reached down beside him and pulled up a handful of french fries from a bag on the floor. He munched on them mechanically.

Maury Povich came on.

He was, Dart Man thought, a weird-looking dude.

He had eyes like the devil, and a deep voice. He always looked like he just woke up.

You could tell from the way Maury talked that he didn't like sluts, either. His Chinese eyes would narrow even more than they were to begin with when he talked about them. He bet Maury wouldn't mind firing a few darts to teach some lessons.

He sucked deeply on the cigarillo.

He thought it would be great if he could do to sluts what they used to do in a lot of countries. Take their clothes off and throw them into a volcano and let the hot lava take care of their sluttish bodies. It was too bad that was no longer done.

The first segment came on. It was about a little kid who would go around yelling the Bible.

Dart Man wasn't interested. There were no women in it.

His interest level spiked considerably during the commercial. There were plenty of bad girls on the commercials, dressed in all kinds of things that showed what they were.

He wished he could get at them. He would teach those filthy pigs a lesson. But they were all away in Florida, or somewhere, so he couldn't get at them.

Dart Man's interest level stayed high when Maury announced the second segment. It was a case of marital infidelity and murder . . . and flashed on the screen was a bunch of quick photos, including a woman in a bikini . . .

Dart Man sucked very deeply on the cigarillo and leaned forward in the chair.

Maury talked about how the woman in the bikini was such a slut. She had fucked a man who had been a teacher and then killed his wife.

They showed a picture of her. She was in a pink bathing suit. She had the body of a slut. A filthy fucking slut.

The man got up and walked over to the TV. He was half erect. He turned it off.

He went over to the only closet in the room and opened the door. He reached down and took out a shoe box from beneath a pile of clothes and other stuff on the floor.

He set the box on top of the television and opened it. Inside were his darts, perhaps fifty in all, and his sturdy plastic straw.

He carefully picked up one of the darts and looked at it in the light. He bunched up the "feathers" and pushed the dart into the straw. He lay the weapon on the TV and returned the box to the closet. A few minutes later, he was on the street prowling with the weapon in his coat pocket.

CHAPTER 21

Dart Man got on the subway at 145th Street and took the train down to the area around New York University. He knew that a lot of sluts hung around Washington

Square Park and the school. Maybe the slut who killed her loverboy's wife would be there, too.

It was a warm, pleasant night and the area around the monument was crowded. People were talking and laughing and playing musical instruments.

Dart Man hardly noticed. His eyes scanned from ass to ass, looking for the right one.

The thought of firing a dart here was getting him very excited, but he sensed that it was very dangerous. There were lots of people around. Young people. If one saw him do it, they could catch him. He had to be very careful.

Then he spotted a blond woman in short pink pants. She was walking along on one of the streets around the park. Quickly, he trotted over until he was about five yards behind her.

His eyes fixed on her buttocks. The cheeks of her behind raised and lowered rhythmically. It was as if her ass were an obscene machine mocking him and trying to make him feel small. He was furious.

He pictured himself firing the dart into her left buttock, and imagined the pain and humiliation she would suffer. Then he would fire darts into both eyes.

He felt a tickling and swelling in his scrotum. He realized that he was sweating.

He glanced this way and that. It was still crowded and very dangerous. His picture had been in all the papers and on TV. He could get caught.

He was just about to fire when a big, young dark-haired guy joined the woman and walked beside her. She smiled up at him. She knew him.

Dart Man felt deflated and enraged. He would have liked to hurt both of them.

He scanned desperately for someone else. No one. It was a special ass he sought, not just any ass.

He got to the corner and thought that maybe he should go where other sluts were.

He looked down the block and saw a cluster of people. A bunch of motorcycles were parked side by side facing the curb.

Slowly, he ambled toward the group.

As he got closer he saw a group of bikers clustered on the corner. They were men and women, all in leather and denim and with stringy hair and bandannas and tattoos. Even some of the women had tattoos. Most of them were drinking from cans wrapped in paper bags. Everyone was smoking.

They were of all shapes and sizes. Some men had beer bellies, but others were slim. Most of the men were heavily muscled.

The women were a mixed group, some fat, some not fat. Everybody was tan and looked greasy, as if they had not bathed in weeks.

A couple of the bikers idly glanced at him as he went by.

There were, he saw, at least two sluts with jutting asses, but there was no way he could risk a shot. There were bushes, but even if he took a shot from behind there, they might still catch him.

He carried a knife, but he knew he would be no match for them.

Then, near the corner, he saw her. She was sitting

on a low concrete fence, smoking. She glanced his way and took a deep drag. Marijuana.

She was clearly a slut, and it was confirmed when she stood up. She had a slut's ass. Her upper arms were covered with tattoos, and she wore earrings and had dark hair held to her head with a polka-dotted bandanna.

She was pure slut, and he knew that he would take her, no matter what the risk. He hated her.

As he went by, he did not look at her, even though she was facing his direction. There was no one nearby.

He extracted his dart gun from his pocket and turned around slowly as he passed. She had started walking the other way. There were people coming toward him, but they were at least twenty yards away.

His rage was palpable. He was almost fully erect.

He inhaled and blew hard through the straw. The dart spiraled through the air. A moment later, as he turned, he heard her.

"What the fuck!"

He turned back. The slut was fingering her ass, trying to see what was there. He felt relieved and triumphant, but alert. He kept moving.

She yelled out.

"Johnny! Dave! C'mere!"

Dart Man knew it was dangerous to stay, and when he turned back he realized just how dangerous it was.

The slut was pointing in his direction, and then the two beefy bikers started to walk his way.

He took off at a sprint. He heard yelling and commotion behind him.

CHAPTER 22

Benton and two other task force detectives interviewed the biker woman, or "Mama," as she was known in the group. Her name was Lurleen Adams and she lived in Providence, Rhode Island. She was a member of the "Brood Club." They were just passing through.

The detectives discovered she was a tough piece of work. Foul-mouthed and hard-bitten, she looked thirty, going on fifty. They were surprised to find out she was only twenty-two.

She explained that she had gotten a good look at the "little nigger" who blew the dart at her. When shown the composite drawing, she exclaimed, "That's the little jerkweed!"

She had only one regret.

"We got to move on," she said, "or else we would spend some time hunting down that pathetic little motherfucker. And spank him. He's a bad boy. Probably a fag, too."

She also talked to the media, and repeated the story of the pathetic little jerkweed.

Benton and seven other cops spent three hours canvassing the Washington Square area, talking with people who had observed the incident and had seen the little black guy running away.

They gathered a lot of data, but it all just seemed to confirm that the perp was Dart Man.

They went back to task force headquarters at One Police Plaza, discussed briefly what they had—nothing, really—and then dispersed.

George Benton was a great believer in doing his homework on a case. A long time ago, when he had first become a detective, an old-time homicide cop had given him a philosophy he lived by: GOYAKOD, which meant "get off your ass and knock on doors."

There was nothing that could take the place of working hard and knocking on doors. Much of the time it was discouraging. He would be standing in a hallway some dreary winter night, after knocking on fifty or a hundred doors with no results, and it seemed like he would never get anywhere.

Then, the next door he knocked on would open and the person inside would give him a lead and he would be off and running.

Doing your homework also included doing headwork. This meant poring over the DD-5s, which were the written reports of what each of the detectives had done each day. You tried to find patterns and links between cases.

When he got back to the apartment from the crime scene, he did just that.

The paperwork on the Dart Man case had piled up. There were the DD-5s from the detectives in the original precincts as well as reports from the task force.

Benton had a stack of papers three inches high to get through.

He began around midnight, and it was dawn when he was through.

He did not find any new leads. The reports did clarify what he already knew, and he perhaps had a better sense of who Dart Man was and how he operated. Sometimes case details would seep down into the unconscious, only to emerge at the most opportune time.

The attacks occurred in Brooklyn, Manhattan, and the Bronx. All occurred before 10:00 A.M. and after 5:00 P.M., except the latest, which was about 8:30 P.M.

Benton arrived at the same conclusion as before: the perp had a regular job, or was otherwise occupied between ten and five.

He was a small black man estimated to be in his mid-thirties. He was thin and quick on his feet. One of the victims had pursued him, and the bikers had taken off after him.

Another victim, Colleen McKay, had said that she smelled something sweet, like perfume. She thought she knew the name of it but couldn't quite place it.

Linda Wolosky also said that she smelled something sweet and that maybe it was perfume.

The profile of the victim was clearly established. She was young and had dark hair and eyes and a sexy figure featuring a prominent behind.

The attacks, except for Colleen McKay's, appeared to be random. Benton could not accept coincidence as an explanation for that. Colleen was stalked.

And why her? Maybe he saw her on TV or something.

Benton got to bed about six-thirty in the morning. Ellen was there. He put his arms around her and nestled his face into her neck. Within seconds all thoughts of the case faded and he was asleep.

Chapter 23

The day after the attack on the biker woman, Dart Man sat down in his battered upholstered chair to watch the evening news. He wondered if they would have the slut on. He wondered if she would be crying.

The door to his room was closed, but he could hear his aunt puttering around in the next room, preparing to go to work.

Dart Man was very relaxed and feeling good. Empty. He always felt like this after showing one of the sluts what he could do. He would think of how powerful he was. He would masturbate. His fantasy of penetrating soft flesh was inseparable from firing the dart. It was as if the dart hung down between his legs.

Immediately after an attack, he didn't think too much about sluts. He would think about what he was going to eat, and he would see how the Mets were doing. Or he would watch TV. He liked the game shows, and even when the sluts came on, it didn't bother him if it had been a short time since he had punished one of them.

As time went by, his concentration would become poor. Anxiety would build. Then he would turn inward and start thinking about the sluts and get angrier and angrier as the days passed.

He would masturbate violently as he pictured himself penetrating sluts, and that would relieve the anger and anxiety. After a while that didn't work. He had to do something.

He lit a cigarillo and dragged deeply. The smoke poured out his thin nose. He felt like a man of the world.

The news came on with a man and a woman. Dart Man didn't know if she was a slut because he couldn't see her body. She just had the face of an older lady trying to look younger.

They went back and forth. The man would say something, and then the woman would say something. It was like playing Ping-Pong with words.

They were talking about a fire in an Atlantic City nursing home in which eleven residents had been overcome and five killed. It meant as much to Dart Man as a fire in a fireplace would.

Then they came to him. He dragged deeply and leaned forward. They talked about yet another attack in the Dart Man case that was terrorizing women in the midtown area as well as the other boroughs.

The statement suffused Dart Man with pleasure. He felt great.

"The latest victim," the woman announcer said,

"was Lurleen Adams, from Providence, Rhode Island who was attacked at about eight-thirty last night in Washington Square Park by the small black man who fits the description of Dart Man."

Then they had an interview with the slut. She had stringy hair, bad teeth, and the tattoo of a snake on her right cheek. He knew she had a powerful ass.

"How do you feel about this?" the announcer asked. "Is this going to keep you from visiting New York in the future?"

Lurleen sneered. "No [bleep] way," she said, "this guy doesn't scare me. He's just a pip-squeak. Probably afraid of girls . . ."

The statement made Dart Man go breathless, then blank. Her mouth was moving, but all he could hear was "pip-squeak."

Pip-squeak.

Pip-squeak.

Pip-squeak.

Pip-squeak.

He sat there, almost hyperventilating.

He got up and walked toward the TV. He was quivering. He felt like crying.

He grabbed a heavy glass ashtray, and, just before he was about to throw it into the picture tube, he pivoted and threw it against the wall. It shattered.

The newscaster had gone on to something else.

The door to his room flew open. Standing in the doorway was a heavyset black woman dressed in medical whites.

"Stewart," she said, her eyes wide, "what's the matter? You okay?"

He said nothing.

Aunt Martha was used to outbursts like this. Stewart had had what Aunt Martha called "spells" since he had gotten out of Central Islip Psychiatric. He was harmless and this was rare but it still upset her.

Aunt Martha felt so sorry for Stewart. If only his mother, her sister Gloria, hadn't been sick. But she had been. It was a curse that passed from one generation to another. All Martha could do was pray for Stewart, and she did it often.

"I'll see you later, honey," she said, and closed the door.

Stewart stood there, quivering with rage.

Three hours later Stewart was still in his room and he was thinking about the slut on TV. She was such a slut. She called him a name. A bad name.

She was such a filthy dirty slut of a cunt. Her big ass challenged and mocked him. She called him a pipsqueak. He could kill her and cut her ass off.

Almost mechanically, his jaw muscles working, he went to the closet and took out the shoe box. He reached in and carefully removed all the darts and the straws he had made.

He went into the bathroom. Slowly and methodically, he cut the straws in half and dropped them down into the toilet and flushed. They all went down.

Then he dropped the darts into the toilet and also flushed them away.

He looked at his face in the mirror. He was sweating and his eyes were bloodshot and fierce. Something screamed inside him, but the only indication was a certain brightness in his eyes. The image pleased him.

Chapter 24

Frankenstein walked down Mulberry Street, a quaint street in an area known as Little Italy, which was unchanged physically—it was lined with small apartment buildings and stores selling Italian products—from the way it looked fifty years ago. However, ethnically things were very different. So many Chinese had moved into the area and taken over the small businesses that some people suggested its name be changed to Little Hong Kong.

"God works in strange ways," Piccolo said to Howie after they set up the meet. "But what the fuck. He does have two good points. He's good-looking and he's a guinea."

Piccolo was speaking of Aniello "Neil" Falco, the boss of the Falco family, the largest in New York, and therefore the most powerful in America. He was capo di tutti capi, the Godfather.

Falco had achieved his esteemed position by having nine bullets pumped into the head of his former boss, Paul "the Weasel" Pappallardo. Of course, Falco never acted alone. He was no cowboy, and he was shrewd, which was why he was alive at the age of forty-five. The killing of Pappallardo had been approved by the heads of two of the four other major families. The two others had not objected; "went along," according to Falco's own account.

In the two years since his ex-boss's life had leaked out of him outside a steak house where he was to dine, Falco had become a media darling, though he didn't court the media, like his distant cousin Joe Columbo. This could be unhealthy, as Joe Columbo's survivors were to learn. The Mafia did not like attention drawn to itself, or maybe it was simple jealousy.

Falco was a handsome man with a thick shock of graying hair combed straight back. His features were straight and well-defined, he had a nice toothy smile and smallish eyes with a twinkle in them. One undercover cop called it a murderous twinkle.

He was a spiffy dresser, though he tended to overdress. He looked like he had walked straight out of a Damon Runyon story. But Falco was hardly the Runyonesque figure he appeared to be. One U.S. Attorney said, "He didn't get where he is by being Mr. Roberts." And to hear him talk was to hear a man who could not express himself without the word fuck. It was a verbal clue to the fires that raged within him.

Frankenstein were going to a social club where Neil Falco and some of his top people went to get away from their wives, to play some cards, maybe have a friendly little dice game, drink some wine and plan their next illegal exercise.

The government was always trying to wire these places, and whenever anyone talked, the assumption was that they were being taped, though Falco regularly had it swept for bugs. They spoke mostly in code. Or they talked with the water or the radio on loudly. The most important conversations occurred in the bathroom as the toilet was repeatedly flushed.

Frankenstein knew Louis Gaggi, a *caporegime* in Falco's family, and he had approached the big man with the request. Falco's reply was to visit him at the club and they would jaw about it.

The club was an ordinary store with a painted plateglass window, which read:

MULBERRY ROD, GUN AND SPORTS CLUB
Friends Welcome

Stein looked at Piccolo. "I didn't know," he said, "they were doing people with fishing rods now."

Piccolo laughed.

Two burly, dark-haired, dark-eyed men who had been standing nearby approached Frankenstein as they slowed down in front of the club.

"Piccolo?" one of them said, eyes darting from one to the other.

"Yeah, I'm Frank Piccolo."

He smiled, though there was no mirth in it.

"Neil's inside."

Inside, there were three or four tables, one occupied with a group of people playing cards. Some of the card players glanced up idly, then went back to their game.

There was a wet bar on one side of the room, which was deserted, and also a professional barber's chair. Frankenstein had heard that Falco liked to get his hair trimmed once a week.

There was also a louver door leading to a back room. A man emerged. He was small, hawk-faced, and pockmarked. He looked familiar to Piccolo, and then the detective realized why. He had seen him in the papers and on TV, close to or trailing Falco. He was probably a bodyguard.

He opened the door and Frankenstein went inside. There was a round table. Falco was sitting at it, flanked by a young guy and an older one. Frankenstein recognized the younger guy, who wore a black T-shirt and was built like a weight lifter. He resembled Falco, except for the thick ridge of bone over his eyes that gave him a slightly apelike look. The looks were not a coincidence. His name was Neil, Jr., and he was Neil Falco's oldest son. He had a reputation just as nasty as Neil, Srs.', but not as slick.

The older guy was sucking on a cigarette, and they recognized him as Joe Corona, consigliere to four godfathers spanning four decades. You had to marvel at this guy's capacity for survival.

Falco, dressed in a light satin shirt open at the throat to reveal a gold chain and—what else?—a crucifix, stood up and smiled. He shook hands with both of them and then made the introductions.

He invited them to sit down.

"Some wine?"

"Yeah," Piccolo said, "and leave the bottle."

Falco smiled. Stein declined. He thought it unlikely they had San Pellegrino here. He asked. They did.

Falco, Sr. inquired as to how their job was going while the guy who let them in went for the drinks. Frankenstein didn't know what to ask him. What do you ask? How are your rubouts going?

But they did manage to comment on the weather, to make the situation as natural as possible. Neil, Sr. was a charming kind of guy. Piccolo and Stein both got the feeling that Falco, Jr. would kill you as quick as he would piss on you. Joe Corona looked friendly; you couldn't tell what he was thinking.

Corona lit a cigarette and Piccolo took his lead, and smiled.

"So," Falco said, "Louis said I might be able to help you guys in some way."

"That's right," Piccolo said, "we need help."

"We're trying to get a line on this crash-and-dash gang that's been working Manhattan. We've had no luck."

Falco smiled a little.

"Oh yeah, those fucking wallos. Ballsy fucking kids. You know who they are."

"Yeah," Piccolo said, "we know. The Gazzas."

"Why don't you just set 'em up. Cops do that, right?"

Everybody laughed hard. Do bears shit in the woods?

"Hey, Neil—may I call you Neil?" Piccolo asked. It was what they called him when they saved his life, so it should still be good.

Falco nodded.

"We don't engage in activities like that. We go by the book."

"Yeah," Falco smiled, "I know." Then he chortled. "So how can I help you?"

"We want to know," Stein said, "who they're laying the swag off on."

"I see," Falco said. "Once you know that, maybe you can do something with the fence."

"You got it," Piccolo said. Falco was a very sharp dude indeed.

Falco looked from left to right.

"Anything to add, Joe?" he said to his consigliere, who shook his head slightly. "Neilly?"

His son added nothing but a brooding sense of violence. "No," he said.

"Okay," Falco said, "I'll see what I can do. And what if I find this fucking guy, what can you offer me?"

There was the slightest focusing of attention by the three mafiosos on Frankenstein.

"You're here, right?" Stein said.

He was referring to the fact that he wasn't in the bone orchard thanks to Frankenstein.

"That's true," Falco said, "but this is big. Once it gets out, if it does, that we're working with cops . . . that creates a bad image. We're taking a big fucking risk."

Frankenstein played along.

"What do you want?"

"My brother Gene's got a little beef that needs to be cleared up."

Frankenstein looked at Falco and wondered what it

was. A little beef to Falco might be that his brother rolled a live grenade into St. Patrick's Cathedral during Easter Sunday Mass.

"He was in a fight with some scumbag in a bar. The guy called him a guinea motherfucker—which you can appreciate, Frank—so Gene busted him up a little."

"What's a little?" Stein said.

"He spent some time in the hospital."

"How many years?" Piccolo said.

Falco and Corona laughed hard. Even Neil, Jr. managed a smile. Or maybe the grimace meant he was trying to shit in his pants.

"No, just a few weeks. But the DA is making a big fucking pasta sauce out of the fucker. He wants to fuck Gene."

Frankenstein knew that Falco was working them. But they would check it out.

"Okay," Piccolo said, "we'll see what we can do. But it's not up to us about Gene. That's the DA's territory."

"I know," Falco said, "we'll see what we can do. Nice seeing you again."

Frankenstein left, and as they went out the door they had the distinct feeling that all eyes were trained on them. It was like having Arabs at a bar mitzvah. Cops made wise guys tense.

CHAPTER 25

The Assistant DA handling the Gene Falco case for the Bronx DA was Arthur Silberstein. He was not enthusiastic.

They spoke in Silberstein's office in the Bronx County Courthouse Building, a massive gray concrete structure that was home to the courts that handled criminal cases generated in the Bronx.

Silberstein was a small man with just a fringe of hair around his head. His brow was furrowed when he spoke. "I don't like the idea of letting this guy walk. We're talking about a career criminal, and a mafioso. A bad guy. A killer. All the Falcos are killers."

Frankenstein were sitting opposite Silberstein, who was ensconced behind a massive desk that emphasized his smallness. They looked at him and said nothing.

"Do you know what Gene Falco tried to do to the victim? Tried to drown him in a toilet. Only the chance entrance of two plainclothes cops saved his life."

Stein spoke. "We know how bad Gene is, but we know also that the Gazzas are killers. One of these times when they go on one of their jobs, someone is going to die. Maybe a kid who gets caught in the crossfire. Maybe an old guy . . ."

"Maybe a pregnant mother," Piccolo said.

Silberstein scowled. Give me a goddamn break, he thought.

"Well," Stein said, "it may not be too farfetched. At least, there is the potential for that."

Silberstein was not impressed. Why should he make a deal for a hood based on the presumption of future violence inflicted upon the innocent?

Piccolo spoke again. "Art, are you familiar with the Gazza brothers?"

"I know they've been causing some problems in some of the other boroughs."

"I would fucking say so," Piccolo said. "They're breaking lots of balls in a lot of precincts. There are a lot of red faces."

"If we can get these guys," Stein said, "it will be a banner day for law enforcement. And if you can get a conviction, I guarantee you'll make a lot of friends. And you won't do your career any harm either."

"I don't care about my career," Silberstein said.

Piccolo looked flatly at him. Right, he thought, and I wouldn't mind having group sex with a herd of water buffalo.

"These guys have done eighty-eight jobs," Piccolo said. "It's going to be a media event. It could help all of us, and maybe keep someone alive—and win one for the good guys."

Silberstein was quiet for a moment. With Falco, he had a bird in hand. This would be taking a risk.

"We can give the deal," he said, "after we indict the Gazza brothers."

"No fucking way," Piccolo said. "Neil Falco won't go for that. He wants a sure thing."

"I don't know," Silberstein said.

Piccolo felt himself getting hot. This little fuck.

"Maybe you should check it with Patterson," Piccolo said.

Silberstein's eyes darted up and fixed on Piccolo.

Patterson was the District Attorney. Silberstein knew what Piccolo was really saying. We'll go over your head.

Silberstein felt his face flush.

"No," he said, "we don't have to do that. We'll go for it. He gives you the name of the fence, we'll reduce the assault charge to a dis con. But I hope to Christ it leads somewhere. We're letting a real bad guy walk."

Frankenstein smiled.

"You won't regret it," Stein said.

An hour later the deal was completed via phone. Falco would come up with the name of the fence or fences. When he did, Silberstein would reduce the charges against his brother.

Now all they could do was wait.

CHAPTER 26

Less than twenty-four hours later, Neil Falco, Sr. got back to Frankenstein with a name and some details on the man behind the name. "No extra charge," Falco said.

Falco told Frankenstein that the Gazza brothers had one fence, and his name was Irwin "The Large" Gold. Gold would take just about anything stolen. He had once taken a load of siphon jet toilets. His marketing system was as good or better than most retail department stores. He could resell the stuff domestically, internationally, or just drop it across the border to Mexico.

Irwin lived in a penthouse on York Avenue just north of New York Hospital overlooking the East River. He was a clever guy, and when Frankenstein threw his name into the computer, it showed he had no yellow sheet. He went through life posing as a diamond merchant, and each day would go to a tiny store, supposedly a wholesale jewelry company, on 47th Street off Madison Avenue in Manhattan.

Frankenstein got a description of him from the DMV, and when they first saw him coming out of his store—they were in a surveillance van down the street—they were surprised.

"Now I know," Piccolo said, "why they call him large and why he lives near New York Hospital. When he has his coronary, it'll be a short trip to emergency."

Gold was immense. Frankenstein figured he was close to four hundred pounds, a balding blob of a man who looked far older than his thirty-nine years. Plus, he smoked. Nice.

"This fucking guy," Piccolo said, "probably has to pay whores double if he does it in the missionary position—half for the lay and half hazard pay for possibly being crushed or suffocated.''

Frankenstein had to decide how to handle the approach. They were eager to work on him, but they didn't want to blow it. Whatever they did, they decided to tell the Midtown South cop, Kenney, later. They didn't want him to try to sneak the collar away from them.

They decided to stay off Gold until the Gazza gang hit again. It wasn't much of a decision because they had nothing else. They figured the Gazzas would ultimately come to Gold, and they would be there when the connection was made.

They told Lawless the truth regarding Falco's involvement, and told Captain Bledsoe they got a tip on Gold from one of their snitches. When the brass called to break his chops, the captain would have some progress to report.

Bledsoe didn't probe where they got the tip. He just wanted to report progress.

It was a good day for Bledsoe the day he learned about the fence. It was also the day he learned the blacks had lifted their boycott of the Korean deli, and his wife had dropped the garlic diet for one featuring chocolate milk shakes. The day was about as good as it got for him.

Three days after they found out that Irwin the Large was the Gazza fence, there was another crash-and-dash caper, at a jewelry store in Brooklyn. It had all the marks of the Gazza boys. The van had been backed in and only the best stuff was taken. The gang members wore masks, and a Monte Carlo was seen speeding away from the scene.

At the scene, Frankenstein told the investigating detectives that they thought the Gazza brothers did it, but no more.

Then they put their plan into action. They started to shadow the Large. Hopefully he would lead them to the promised land.

CHAPTER 27

The night the Gazzas took down the jewelry joint, Frankenstein were in a van about a half block down from the Large's apartment building, watching the entrance. They were hoping one of the Gazza boys would show up. If he did, it certainly wouldn't be with the swag. But he might take Irwin to it, and then it would simply be a matter of following them to the location.

Or, maybe, Irwin would make a house call.

Frankenstein couldn't do the surveillance alone, so they enlisted the aid of two other squad detectives, Arnold Gertz and Ray Flynn. Lawless said that he would also be available if needed.

They watched Gold for three days, and during that time they started to notice a pattern that Gold lived by. At the core of his existence was food.

He would waddle west to First Avenue and 69th Street

and sit himself in a diner. Stein followed him to the diner one day, and Piccolo another. He had ham and eggs . . . and sausage and bacon and toast and pancakes, and milk shakes to wash the food down. All this was followed by several unfiltered cigarettes.

Piccolo only hoped the caper would be done before the guy was.

Then Irwin the Large would taxi over to his office on 47th Street. He would leave around noon to return to his apartment. It was obviously a do-nothing job to cover himself for the IRS.

He would stay in his apartment for the rest of the day, doing his real work by phone.

Around five o'clock he would leave and taxi into midtown. One night he went to an Italian place called Il Cantinori, and the next he went to Docks, a place featuring seafood.

He was in each of the restaurants for over two hours, though no one who tailed him could be sure he was eating. They assumed that he was. And how much could a person eat in two hours . . . a mountain?

The next two days, his pattern was the same.

On the fifth night, he got into a cab outside his apartment and headed downtown. Frankenstein got a little excited. Maybe he was going to the Gazza house.

But that wasn't to be. Gold stopped at a house on Bleecker Street, and fifteen minutes later, he emerged with a blonde who was dressed in what looked like a white sausage skin and was young enough to be his daughter. They got in the cab and then went to Il Cantinori.

This time he was out in an hour and a half, and they

took a cab back to his apartment. No doubt other appetites had been stimulated.

The cops watched until dawn, but the blond young lady did not come out until about nine o'clock, when she emerged with Gold. He put her in a cab, then took a cab to the office.

These activities were photographed, and the film was rushed down to central ID for developing, to see if they could get a make on her. You never knew what someone's identity might reveal.

The woman had no yellow sheet. Later, if necessary, they would check her further.

On the next night the same thing happened, more or less. Gold left his apartment, took a cab to the Village and picked up a girl, and then went out to dinner with her, took her back to his apartment and did not emerge for the rest of the night.

This time the girl was a brunette, and she had, in Piccolo's opinion, "bigger tits" than the girl of the night before.

On the morning of the seventh day, Frankenstein followed Gold, as usual, to his wholesale jewelry store on 47th Street. As they did, they wondered how long Lawless was going to allow the surveillance to continue. The case was important, but there were other cases starting to pile up in the precinct.

Frankenstein knew, too, that the longer they shadowed this guy, the more likely it was they'd take a burn. Frankenstein and the other cops were experienced on stakeout work, but after awhile a "surveillee" would sense he was being watched and the burn would be inevitable.

As the huge form of Gold disappeared into his store, Piccolo commented to Stein, "I hope something happens soon."

"Amen," said his partner.

CHAPTER 28

That night Gold dramatically broke the pattern.

It was about two in the morning, and Frankenstein were sitting in Piccolo's black Trans Am. Stein was in the front passenger seat and Piccolo was in the back. It was an old surveillance trick. Someone looking in the vehicle might assume that the people in it were passengers waiting for the driver to show up.

Gold emerged from his apartment building and stood there a couple of minutes, smoking and looking up the street toward them. The Trans Am was parked behind another car, but for a while they thought they might have been spotted.

At about 2:05 they heard wheels squealing behind them. When it went by, their hopes soared. It was a maroon-colored 1979 Monte Carlo in mint condition.

It stopped in front of Gold's building and he got in. A few moments later it was on its way down the block, and so were Frankenstein.

Stein was driving.

"I hope this guy doesn't take off," Stein said. He knew the Gazzas' reputation for being heavy on the pedal. If Stein had to speed to follow him, then the chances of taking a burn were high. They were high anyway, because they were trailing a car at this hour of the morning and there were not many other cars on the street.

Fortunately, the Monte Carlo was driven at a legal pace, and Frankenstein kept well behind.

"So far," Piccolo said, dragging on a cigarette, "so fucking good."

The car hit the East River Drive going downtown, and that was fine with Frankenstein. There were other cars on the highway and they provided some cover.

They followed the Monte Carlo through the Queens-Midtown Tunnel, then through a ganglion of blocks until they were in Long Island City, an area of Queens just across the river from New York City, mainly consisting of blocks and blocks of factories and warehouses. It looked like the industrial revolution landed there and never left, and no one ever bothered to modernize or maintain the buildings.

Just after they exited the tunnel, the Monte Carlo's brake lights went on; it eased up in front of a brick warehouse on a corner and stopped. Frankenstein stopped, too, observing the action four blocks away.

The driver got out and then Gold unloaded. There was not a lot of light, but the driver appeared to have a shock of dark hair, the main feature of Anthony Gazza.

Gold, lumbering slowly along, followed Gazza into the building.

Frankenstein started the car again and slowly drove down one block and then a second, stopping about fifty yards from the Monte Carlo.

Piccolo and Stein looked at each other.

"Let's take some hardware," Piccolo said.

Stein turned around and reached down on the floor of the rear seat. He came up with two 12-gauge, pump-action shotguns. He was packing a 9mm Glock, and Piccolo had a .357 Magnum as well as a Glock.

They got out of the car and trotted down the street. There didn't seem to be any way their approach could be observed. The street was empty, a typical factory/warehouse area in the wee hours of the morning, peopled only by cats, rats, the homeless, or someone looking for a score.

There were windows maybe eight feet off the ground in the front, as well as on the side of the building. Frankenstein trotted over to the side. The windows were too high to peek through unless you were ten feet tall.

They lay the hardware against the wall and Stein stood against it under one of the windows. Piccolo climbed up until he was crouched on his shoulders, then slowly stood up the rest of the way and looked in.

He took a ten-second look and that was enough. He jumped down.

"All fucking there. And they got some furs right out in the fucking open."

"Who'd you see?"

"Both Gazzas, Gold, and two other gang guys."

"Call for backup?"

"Fuck no," Piccolo said.

The Gazzas were known as shooters.

"Vests."

"Naw," Piccolo said, "let's give 'em a fucking chance."

They picked up the shotguns and went around to the front of the building.

There was an overhead door, and right next to it, a regular door.

Stein tried the knob and was surprised when it turned. The door was open. He glanced at Piccolo.

He pushed the door open slowly. It made no sound.

Directly ahead were some crates piled high. They could not see anyone, but they could faintly hear talking.

They closed the door behind them and walked as quietly as possible down the hall created by the space between the front wall and the crates. They were side by side, shotguns extended.

After looking at each other, they stepped beyond the crates into the open.

They scanned the scene and were not spotted for a moment. It was an important moment.

"Freeze or die, motherfuckers!" Piccolo yelled. "Hands on your fucking skulls."

Directly in front were the Gazza brothers, Rocky Lumaghi, and Jeff Siegel.

Anthony Gazza made a quick motion to go for a piece in a shoulder holster, and Piccolo yelled, "Go ahead, Anthony!"

Anthony stopped and put his hands on his head.

Frankenstein were jubilant. They knew they had them—the Gazza gang, the fence, and the evidence, all right here.

"You or me?" Piccolo said.

"I'll cover you."

"Lay down on the floor, hands behind your back," Piccolo said. They all complied, but Piccolo wondered if Irwin the Large was going to be able to get back up.

Piccolo took his handcuffs and then Stein's and quickly and expertly cuffed their hands behind their backs, also relieving them of their hardware. Irwin carried nothing—except a hugh wad of hundred dollar bills.

"Stay there," Piccolo said.

Without further ado, Piccolo went outside and ran down the block to the car. He radioed for backup. They would be there within minutes.

All they could do now was wait.

Piccolo went back to the warehouse and took his place beside Howie.

Irwin the Large looked white.

"Irwin," Piccolo said, "look at it this way. Where you're going, you can go on a diet, and you don't have to worry about being fucked. You'll have it made."

Slim, the thin, stringy-haired van driver was on the can in a small bathroom in the back of the warehouse when Frankenstein broke in, and he understood right away what was going down.

He had a Beretta with him, and figured he could come out and maybe get them under the gun, but he didn't know how many there were, and he fucking didn't want to get in a shootout with cops.

So Slim did the next best thing. He interrupted his business, pried open the ancient bathroom window, climbed out, and trotted off into the night.

Chapter 29

A week after they collared the Gazza group, Assistant District Attorney Arthur Silberstein insisted on taking Frankenstein out to dinner. He took them to a little Italian place on Arthur Avenue, and over the entrée told them some good news.

Irwin the Large had flipped, and the way he was talking, it was highly unlikely that the Gazzas would not breathe free air until they were old men.

"We got the proceeds of the robbery and we got details on other robberies. Plus you guys caught them with their pants down. We got them good. It's just great."

They spent three hours at the restaurant, and Silberstein got a little tipsy and was driven home by Frankenstein. He would have a hangover, but it was worth it. It was the biggest case of his career and it would do a lot for him. He admitted, in his cups, that he had his eye on Patterson's job. Ever since he was a little boy he had wanted to do something great.

"And I'll never forget you guys," he said, "you're the greatest cops that ever lived."

"At least," Stein said later, "he's not a man who exaggerates."

In his office, Captain Bledsoe was in good spirits. He smiled frequently, and actually said hello to the men he met.

The source of his joy was not just the Gazza squeal, but a call he had received earlier in the day from Chief Slaughter.

Slaughter had congratulated him on solving a "thorny case that has bothered the department for years," and getting the "perps out of the newspapers and in jail where they belong."

And he had finished his truly inspirational call by saying that downtown was very appreciative of what Bledsoe's detectives had done, and he had done himself a world of good.

On top of this, Bledsoe could now breathe the air in his own house.

Frankenstein were feeling pretty good, too. They had not only destroyed the gang, but they had a good mark on their record—a nice change—and had made Lawless look good. Plus, they had made a good deal with Falco, and even had something of a relationship. Should the need ever arise, they had credibility.

More, they had paid high praise to Kenney and his squad, saying that without them the collar would not have been made. Kenney and his cops basked in the glow, and that also cemented a good relationship.

Finally, and most important, they had done a good job, and justice would be served for those who had been ripped off by the Gazzas. People would be safer because of the job they had done. They never got cynical or joked about that. Before everything, Frankenstein wanted to do their job well. And they had.

In a way, Frankenstein thought, it was one of the easiest squeals they had ever worked. Just a few weeks, really. And such quick success on a case that other cops had not been able to clear in years. It was almost unbelievable.

There was only one loose end—this Slim guy. He was nowhere to be found, and since the Gazzas weren't talking, Frankenstein knew that they had to get lucky. Someone was going to have to pick him up on an APB.

They figured he would be. Irwin the Large told Silberstein that Slim was not a thinker or a planner; he was just a driver. He should not be a problem, and eventually they would pick him up.

CHAPTER 30

Lurleen Adams, biker mama, was in her glory. Her story had been all over the media, and a number of people stopped to ask for her autograph, which she had given. Jeff, her old man, had also paid some extra attention to her. It was good publicity for her and the Brood. And they had a lot of laughs about it. One of the gang members said, "Lurleen's ass has been in every home in America."

Lurleen was down at the same spot in Washington Square Park where she had been attacked. A bunch of others from the Brood were there, too. They were doing what they usually did: drinking beer, chewing the fat, and working on their bikes.

Lurleen was looking forward to something else. In a few days the entire Brood would be leaving for an all-day drive up to Newton, New Hampshire, and the annual bike club convention.

This kind of thing was a gas and a half. There were bike races, parties, and they got to meet a lot of their friends—and enemies—from other clubs. The fair was more or less a truce time, but it was nice just ragging on some of the bad guys.

The Brood would also be bigger by the time it returned to their home base, which was actually a private home on Stuyvesant Avenue in Providence. There were always biker groupies who would want to trail along, and there were always horny guys who would bring them back down. Some would stay and be initiated into the the Brood, while some would go their own way.

Lurleen, dressed in leather and chains, was sitting on the concrete fencing that surrounded the park. She idly sipped a beer, occasionally sucked on a roach. She was feeling good.

Dart Man was on a roof of a five-story apartment building directly across the street.

He had been watching Lurleen for half an hour, waiting for his chance. He tried to keep calm, but he wasn't calm. He was smoking constantly, angry and scared at the same time.

He needed to get a shot at her ass, but he hadn't been able to—yet.

Now, he watched her get up. She had finished her beer and walked away from the fencing. She tossed the empty into a garbage can, then went to an ice chest and got another.

She stood there, the twin boulders of her ass jutting out, the leather stretched taut, reflecting the streetlight.

For Dart Man, all sound faded, and there was just her and him.

She started to walk away. It was now or never. He held her in his sights and squeezed off a shot—and it wasn't a needle.

He missed, but Lurleen fell. He had hit her in the neck.

He watched for a moment, squeezing his eyes pleasurably, and then trotted across the roof with rifle in hand. He jumped a low brick wall and continued until he was four rooftops over. Then, just before descending, he wrapped the rifle in a length of carpet.

He heard screaming up the street, and walked calmly in the opposite direction.

Chapter 31

Lurleen Adams was rushed to St. Vincent's Hospital on Seventh Avenue and Twelfth Street, one of the better hospitals in New York City.

The emergency ward doctors worked on her for over an hour, and finally announced that the dart used, a half-inch-long, pointed piece of steel about a quarter inch in diameter, had not done serious damage. There had been considerable bleeding, but the dart had missed all of the arteries. Lurleen Adams was in serious but stable condition and the prognosis was good.

Within half an hour of the assault, there were six mobile TV crews at the hospital and site of the assault. Both places were also awash with cops, and throngs of the curious gathered.

A rumor spread that the victim had died, but this was quashed by police.

The news media loved it. This was a brutal assault bound to send chills of fear throughout the city, particularly among women. Dart Man had been elevated from a menace to a serious danger. The city was going to have to cope with a full-blown psycho. No one was disclosing exactly what Lurleen Adams had been shot with—but a sewing needle didn't put you in ICU.

If there was doubt in anyone's mind that the perp was

Dart Man, that was disabused by police spokesperson Colleen McKay. She announced that a small black man fitting the description of Dart Man had been spotted close to the scene but moving rapidly away from it.

The task force descended on the scene en masse. It wasn't long before Benton and another cop, named Luther, discovered Dart Man had shot at Lurleen from the roof of the apartment building across the street. The dart was .177 caliber, and a rifle was used. The dart could have been shot with a .22-cartridge or carbon dioxide rifle, and they figured it was carbon dioxide because no one heard the sound of gunfire.

It was a powerful weapon, and up close could go halfway into a two-by-four. Luckily for Lurleen, the angle of her neck was such that the dart went right through it.

But the implication was grim. She could easily have been killed or had an eye knocked out.

They took the stairs to the roof, and there was no question where the shooter had set himself up. He left five dark cigarillo butts mashed into the roof at the exact spot, and when Benton shone his light on the area, there were the slightest scuff marks on the tar paper.

Benton and Luther sighted down to the park.

"Not that difficult a shot with a dart rifle," Benton said. "They're accurate up to about seventy-five yards."

"Based on that, he should have hit her bottom."

"If, in fact, that's what he was aiming for."

Luther nodded. If he was aiming for a vital part . . .

Benton took a clear plastic bag from a pocket and carefully coaxed the cigarillo butts into it.

"He was here," Benton said, "at least an hour."

"I can't picture him coming up in the light. So he probably came about nine."

Benton nodded.

It wasn't hard to figure which way he had left. He had been spotted four blocks from the park. He probably took the stairway of another building down.

Tomorrow they would canvass to see if anyone had seen anything.

Benton contacted Forensics, who came up and tried to lift prints off the tile roof edging. The photographer came and shot a variety of eight-by-ten color shots.

They worked the street scene, talking to bikers and others in the area. No one had seen anything, except a woman walking her dog who had looked up on the rooftop and seen "like a silhouette" of someone up there but thought nothing of it.

Around midnight they got word from St. Vincent's that Lurleen Adams was going to be all right.

No thanks to Dart Man, Benton thought. She had just been lucky.

CHAPTER 32

Ellen was up when Benton got home around one in the morning. She had made a batch of homemade ice cream, and they each had a bowl of it at the kitchen table.

She had heard all the details of the Dart Man attack on television.

"I'm really concerned about it," he said. "I don't know where it's going to end."

"I'm not surprised," she said. "I figured it could go this way."

"Really? You didn't mention that when we last spoke about it."

"It was just a theory," she said, "and I figured, why tell you? You couldn't do any more about it than you're already doing. I didn't see the point."

Benton nodded. In other words, he thought, she didn't want to worry him. Because he did worry about cases. He didn't know if that was neurotic or not, but he took them personally.

"Why do you think he did it? I mean escalated it?"

"This biker woman rubbed salt in his wounds. I think she called him a 'pip-squeak.' Unconsciously, and sometimes consciously, I would guess that's the way he views himself. Small and inadequate. To disprove that to himself, he had to show how powerful and potent he was. It enraged him."

Benton smiled. "So he used an air gun instead of a straw."

"That's right, I think."

"Why do people get so crazy when they feel that way?" Benton asked. "I mean—" He paused to spoon some ice cream into his mouth, because it was hard to say. "—I remember when I had my breakdown. I felt helpless and alone. I think my basic urge to survive was there, but I was terrified I wouldn't make it."

"I think that's right on the money," Ellen said. "This biker told Dart Man that he wasn't adequate. It's a gruesome feeling, so we have to take action against it. The new, escalated assault is the way he did it. He shot down the thing—the symbol."

"Why didn't he just hit her with a needle? Why wasn't that enough?"

"I think," Ellen said, "because the assault on his psyche was too accurate. It required not a minor response, but a major one."

Benton spooned the last of the ice cream into his mouth. "That was delicious."

"I know," Ellen said, and smiled.

Benton smiled back.

"I have no insecurities about my ice cream," she added.

Benton laughed. He got up, went around, and kissed her on the cheek.

"Want to sit on the couch?"

"Sure," she said, "but only if you promise to assault me."

"I promise."

Ellen put the dishes in the sink and ran water into them. Then she joined Benton in the living room on the couch. The momentary parting had made him pensive. He was focusing on Dart Man again.

"He'll do it again, right?" he asked.

"I think so."

"Will he go back and hit one of the original victims?"

"That's a possibility. He might be fantasizing that they're all in league against him. I don't know."

"What's your instinct?"

"That he will."

"Who?"

"I don't know."

"With what?"

"The air gun," she said, and paused. "Or worse. That's pure theory, of course."

"Somebody could get killed."

"That wouldn't bother him. Maybe that's been his purpose. To kill. Maybe it would have taken longer if the biker hadn't criticized him—but maybe he would come to it anyway."

Benton reflected for a moment. "I remember how it was with serial murderers," he said. "They almost always start by torturing or killing small animals. People come later."

"That's right," Ellen said.

There was a pause. Benton spoke again.

"What do you think happened to this guy?"

Ellen looked at him. "In a way," she said, her dark eyes full of love, "it's what happened to you. When you were very young, your parents didn't show you they loved you. And parental love is the way we measure ourselves when we're young. Unconsciously, we say to ourselves: if they don't love me, I can't be worth much. I'll bet anything that if you search his background, you'd find a maternal figure with a nice figure, particularly a shapely bottom."

"This is great stuff," Benton said. "It sounds so right."

There was a panel, then Benton's eyes widened. "I have an idea. . . ." he said, his voice trailing off for a moment. "Would you be able to come in and talk to the task force about this?"

"Sure. But won't there be a political problem with the police psychologist?"

"Not really," Benton said, "because we won't tell him."

Ellen laughed.

They sat silent for a moment, and then she looked down at her legs. The robe she had on had slipped apart and showed the inner part of her thigh.

"Look at this," she said, "my robe slipped apart. I hope no one sees my thigh and gets some ideas."

Benton took a deep breath and took off his shirt.

"I hope so, too," he said.

CHAPTER 33

As head of the Dart Man task force, Lieutenant Jim Frey was ready to try just about anything to clear the case. The scrutiny on the case by the media, the brass, and the public was intense. Who was next?

Ellen Stevens came in the following evening to speak. It was an indication of their concern that every member of the force was there, including one guy who came in with the flu.

"My purpose here, tonight," she said after being introduced by Frey, "is to try to give you an understanding of Dart Man and his psyche. This information might help you prevent him from harming someone else."

Ellen sensed that there were questions, but none were forthcoming. She answered a question she thought might be there.

"My premise," she said, "is that he will attack again—and it might very well be someone that he's already attacked. Let me explain."

She went into an explanation of Dart Man's character, much of which she had detailed to Benton.

She said, "The reason I feel he will attack one of the same women is because he will figure they will be on their guard. Being able to do this will shore up his sense of power, of self. He will be able to accomplish it against all the odds, which includes all of you. He's scared of the police, but I'll bet he's very pleased there's a task force arrayed against him."

Liuetenant Frey, who was in the front, raised his hand.

"Dr. Stevens," he said, "let me posit a situation and see if you think it would work."

She nodded.

"Suppose we have somebody pose as one of the victims, or use one of the victims to lure him into an attack? With your help, maybe we could bait him. Get somebody on the tube to call him a 'pip-squeak' or something like that. Then he would come after her. We'd have her all vested up and we'd be waiting. Would it work?"

Ellen was silent for a moment, then nodded.

"I'd give its chances of working in the high ninety percentile," she said. "You could goad him to go after the decoy with a vengeance—"

"Good," Frey cut in.

She shook her head. "But there would be a problem. You never know exactly how he would come. The next time, he might have a regular rifle with him. And, of course, he's clever. He shot that biker from the roof."

There was silence.

"I would say it's extremely risky, and would counsel against it—unless you could create a situation where there's no risk to the decoy."

No one said anything.

"I think all you can do now," she said, "is warn the

women who have already been attacked. Tell them they are in jeopardy, and try to ensure their safety."

Frey nodded. One of the cops stood up.

"You seem to know an awful lot about this guy. Do you know where he is?"

The question got a little laugh.

"No," Ellen said. "George asked me the same thing. You cops are all alike."

That got a good laugh. Then another cop stood up.

"What do you think he will use on the next attack?"

"I don't know," Ellen said. "I do believe the weapon will be no less dangerous than what he used last time."

"In other words, he won't use a needle."

She nodded.

Frey thanked her for her contribution, and asked her if she might be able to speak with them again. She agreed.

For his part, Benton was very proud of Ellen, and, deep inside, still wondered why she cared about him.

Immediately after the meeting broke up, the task force got on the phones and began to contact victims. They were generally successful, but there were a few who could not be reached.

They would be visited in person or have urgent messages left asking them to contact the task force.

Benton did his share of the work. He strongly believed that everything Ellen said was right. He felt that contacting the victims was helping to get them off the tracks before the train inevitably rolled by.

* * *

The next day a reporter for the *News* found two of the victims and did a front-page piece for the daily with the headline: WHO'S NEXT?

The piece also included a typed note that had been left for one victim. It made what had been a worse case, worse. But all the task force could do was what they were already doing, and hope that they could come up with something before Dart Man struck again.

In fact, Dart Man had no intention of attacking anyone. The attack on the biker slut had been very, very satisfying. As he watched the news and read the stories, he felt very important and powerful. When the story appeared about warnings to his previous victims, it made him feel even better. When he walked down the street, he strutted. He could feel his genitals swinging against his underwear, and his mind was as calm as a mountain lake in a postcard.

CHAPTER 34

Frankenstein were back to the usual run of business at Fort Siberia—the murders, robberies, and rapes that were the stuff of their daily business. There was no such thing as a regular tour for them. They worked until they dropped from fatigue. Neither had families to go home to, unless Piccolo's monitor lizard, python, tokay gekko, boa, and wolverine counted as family.

Most of the squeals were drug-related, and Frankenstein were the first to say that what they were doing would not cure the problem, because there were always young punks to take the place of the deceased. But Frankenstein would say that what they did helped hold back the tide of shit to some degree.

Two weeks after they had collared the Gazzas, they were back in the squad room writing up some reports when Joe Puello, a uniformed cop, came into the room.

He knew Piccolo better than Stein, so he spoke to him.

"There's been another crash-and-dash robbery," he said.

"What, where?" Piccolo asked.

"The Concourse and 188th. A small jewelry store."

"Any more details?"

"That's all we got."

Wordlessly, Frankenstein left the room.

On the way to the scene, Frankenstein theorized that a copycat gang had gone into action. The Gazza brothers' capers had been widely publicized, and it was not a surprise that someone else would try it. Cops knew that crimes sometimes ran according to patterns, including mass murders. In the news there would be an account of some guy walking into a Jersey shopping center and opening up on passersby with an Uzi. Then someone would whack his family in Oklahoma, or somebody would climb a tower in Texas with a bunch of guns and go nuts.

There were a lot of fruitcakes out there, as Piccolo

would say, and those fuckers don't need much to set them off.

The jewelry store that had been hit was off the Concourse. Crime scene tape had been strung up, and there was a crowd of ghouls behind the tape.

There were three blue-and-whites on the scene, and it looked disturbingly familiar. A van had battered through the front window.

Piccolo and Stein looked at each other, pinned their shields to their shirts and were waved into the store by one of the cops.

The inside was familiar, too. The jewelry cases had been smashed and there was some jewelry still lined up, as if it had been purposely left behind.

The proprietor, Bernice Allen, was in the back of the store. She was a small black woman whom Frankenstein estimated was in her fifties. They went over to her.

She looked at Stein and Piccolo.

"Look at this place," she said. "Horrible, just horrible."

"Were you covered?" Stein asked.

The woman glanced at Stein sharply.

"Yes, I was covered," she said, "but that's not the point! This is my place. I had rings that were already engraved. I had brooches . . ."

Her eyes had misted a bit.

"I'm Howie Stein, and he's Frank Piccolo," Stein said. "Can you talk with us now?"

Ms. Allen dabbed her eyes and nodded. There was a glint of fire in them. It occurred to both detectives that to run a jewelry store in Fort Siberia you had to have big chops.

"I can talk," she said. "I was on the job. But that doesn't prepare you for being hit—twice. We were heisted once, and now this. The fuckers."

"Where were you on the job?"

"The Four Seven in the Bronx."

"What's missing," Stein said, "and how much?"

"They only took the most valuable stuff," she said. "They knew what to take. Of course."

Frankenstein glanced at one another. Just like the Gazza brothers.

"Do you recall," Stein asked, "anyone coming in here over the past few weeks and asking you questions about the stuff?"

"We get a lot of what we call browsers," she said, "all kinds of people. Buying a piece of jewelry is a major purchase for most people."

Frankenstein nodded.

"Well," Piccolo said, "we were thinking of one person in particular. A young guy with a beautiful head of black hair."

The statement stopped her.

"Yeah," she said, "I sort of remember someone like that."

"When was he in? This week?"

If he had been, Frankenstein would have been thoroughly stumped. Both Gazzas had been in jail since their arrest a month ago. There had been no bail granted.

"No," she said, "it was before that. Maybe five or six weeks ago. He was in a couple of times."

"How was he dressed?" Stein asked.

"Nicely. Very polite. He said, I think, that he was going to be buying a ring for his fiancée."

The time of the robbery, seven P.M., also fit. It was a pure Gazza MO.

"I was wondering," Piccolo said, "if you would have some time to take a look at some photos. We might be able to come up with a suspect."

"I'm getting the feeling this handsome white boy conned my ass. How about right now?"

The Five Three had a special room downstairs where civilians could view photos, or wait, or be questioned. They drove Ms. Allen over to the precinct and put her in the room. Ten minutes later they had a slide projector set up. The screen was already in place.

They showed her what they called a carousel lineup: photos of perps mixed in with nonperps. She picked Anthony Gazza out right away.

"That's him," she said, "definitely. Bad guy?"

"Yes," Piccolo said.

They drove her back to her shop. Forensics had arrived at the store and was working on it. Piccolo asked to see the reports when they were finished.

They went back to the precinct to try to figure out what was going on. When they got there, they saw a message on the board to contact Captain Bledsoe.

"Wonder what he wants," Piccolo said.

They sat at opposite desks and talked about it.

"It's got to be Gazza," Stein said. "I think we can start with that."

"I agree," Piccolo said. "The one guy got away—Slim. He was the only active gang member left. Maybe Gazza did his homework on the job and fed it to him."

"Or maybe there are players here that we don't know about."

"I don't know," Stein said, "as far as we knew, these were it, right?"

Piccolo nodded. "I think we have to redouble our efforts to find Slim," he said. "I think he may have some answers for us."

They got up, left the squad room and headed for Bledsoe's office. They knew he would want to know what the fuck was going on—though he would not exactly phrase it that way. For once it seemed he was asking a reasonable fucking question.

CHAPTER 35

The young Arab on duty at the long-term parking lot at LaGuardia Airport in Queens was not understanding what the guy, an Indian with a towel around his head and a bad accent, was saying.

Something about a smell. A bad smell.

It was midafternoon on a Tuesday, and it was slow. The attendant let the man show him what he was talking about. He locked the booth and followed the Indian through a warren of cars, some of which had been parked there for months, until they got to a gray Ford. It was a hot day, and by the time they got there, both men were sweating heavily.

"Did . . . dis . . . smook?"

"What you talk about?" asked the attendant, whose name was Fouad.

The Indian made a gesture, and Fouad understood right away. The Indian pressed his nostrils closed with a thumb and forefinger of his right hand. Something stunk.

Fouad moved closer to the car and almost gagged. The car was giving off a smell like limburger cheese that had been baking in the sun.

What the fuck, he thought in Arabic.

He tried to determine the origin of the smell. He moved reluctantly toward the rear of the car.

He had found the source of the smell.

Ohh. He got the idea. He ran back to the booth, to the phone.

The airport police pried the trunk open. The body was in very bad shape, with maggots crawling all over it. At first the cops thought it was a female because of the longish brown hair, but further examination showed it was a thin man with numerous tattoos on his arms, chest, and back. He had a wallet on him with a driver's license and some other papers. His name was Roberts. His name was punched into the computer, and it was discovered there was a bench warrant out on him. One of the PA cops called the detectives in the Five Three who were looking for him.

"Where's the body now?" asked Piccolo, who had taken the call at home.

"Bellevue."

Piccolo called the morgue and spoke with Vic Onairuts, an assistant ME and a good friend of the Felony Squad. He was a balding, intense, blue-eyed man with a very dry sense of humor. Once asked to describe his job, he replied, "Quiet."

"Vic, who's going to do the post on this guy?"

"I can, if you want."

"I want."

"Okay, you want to come down?"

"Yeah, when can you do it?"

"Free right now?"

"Sure, me and Howie'll be down in a half hour."

As he did the post, some things were quickly determined by Onairuts, which he told to Piccolo and Stein.

"He was beaten to death. Took a hell of a trimming."

"Somebody bashed his brains in?"

"For starters."

"How long you figure he's been dead?" Stein asked.

This was one of Onairuts's pet peeves. Only on TV could you be precise about the time someone died. There were so many variables—temperature, body condition, site of the body, etc.—that the joke was that the best way to tell what time someone died was to find the person who had last seen him alive, and say he died between the time when he was last seen alive and when he was found.

"I'd say three or four days . . . maybe more."

"He looks like shit," Piccolo said.

"Hey," Onairuts said, "you'd look like shit if you spent four days in the trunk of a car in a hundred-ten-degree heat with flies breeding in your eye sockets."

Piccolo laughed.

"But you do have a point," Onairuts said. "Somebody systematically kicked the crap out of him before applying the coup de grace. He's got four broken ribs, a fractured hyoid bone, broken arm, lacerations, and abrasions galore. He looks like he's been in a car wreck, and he was burned with a cigarette in various places on his body. Tortured."

"Why?" Stein said. "Why? What for? Who'd want to do this?"

"That's your job, Sherlock," Onairuts said.

"This deepens the fucking mystery," Piccolo said. "Why would anyone want to torture him?"

"I have no idea," Onairuts said.

"Anything else?"

"Nothing remarkable. His pathology is normal. He would have lived a long time."

Piccolo and Stein thanked Onairuts and left the morgue.

They stopped in a diner off 27th Street to have coffee and Danish—and try to determine what was going on.

"I have no idea," Piccolo said, "because we got no fucking motive. Without motive, where are we?"

"I also have the feeling that these crash-and-dash jobs are going to continue."

"Bledsoe is also at the nervous norkus stage. We're not going to get any cooperation from him that puts him at any risk."

"I agree. What we got to do is come up with an innovative idea."

"Yeah," Piccolo said, "maybe we could hire somebody with a crystal ball."

CHAPTER 36

When she went to work on Friday morning, a week after the second attack on Lurleen Adams, Linda Wolosky was not terrified, but she was very tense, and she took steps to make sure that she wouldn't be victimized again. She knew that this time she could get hurt very badly—or worse.

Following the advice of the detective who had called, she had been leaving for work at very different times. Her boss at Computer Associates allowed her to come in just about any time she wanted.

Also, she avoided the Fordham train station, and took another train downtown. She walked up to Kingsbridge and took the IRT elevated train and then transferred to the IND at 161st Street and River Avenue. In fact, the

IRT was closer to her home; she had only taken the IND because it meant more exercise.

She also was careful during the day, taking her lunch in the office, and not going on outside breaks. Mr. Benton, the detective she had spoken to, had told her that the chances of Dart Man finding out where she worked were slim. The mental state she was in prompted her to do it anyway.

She also went home at different times of the day, depending upon when she got to work. On the first four days of the week, she had arrived home at four different times.

She was, also, very wired when on the street. She was very aware of who was around—and behind her. She kept her eyes open for a small black man with bushy hair.

Linda also carried a weapon. A girl in the data processing department had approached her and said she was sorry to hear about the attack and the state that this creep had put her in. Would she like to borrow a canister of Mace?

It was illegal, but Linda didn't really care. She didn't think the cops would do much to her if she used it on someone.

On Friday evening she got off the train at around eight-thirty and walked across Kingsbridge Road, a main thoroughfare that was almost as busy as Fordham Road. She went west until she hit University Avenue, which was perhaps five minutes from the train station. Then she started walking south toward the building complex where she lived.

Linda had also followed the detective's advice as far as clothing was concerned. She wore fairly loose-fitting garments, though she did have a figure and could not hide everything completely.

Psychologically, the detective said, "On the chance that he does try to go after you, the loose clothing might send him a different message."

As she walked down University Avenue, a street flanked on one side by a series of five-story buildings and on the other by an immense park, she was well aware that it was a bad area of the neighborhood. She was glad she had worn loose clothing. Walking down this block in tight clothing in the gathering darkness was asking for trouble.

But no trouble came. She let herself into her modern lobby and walked to the elevators. There was no one in the lobby. She glanced around.

She pressed the button for the elevator and waited. It came immediately. The doors opened. She sighed. It was empty. She stepped on and pushed her floor button. The elevator rose.

She got off on her floor, and started toward her door.

When the door to the emergency stairs at the end of the hall opened, she blanched. She was face-to-face with the little black man. He carried a rifle, and started to raise it. She screamed and fainted, falling, just as he fired. The sound of the air gun popped sharply in the confines of the hall.

CHAPTER 37

Miraculously, Dart Man missed Linda Wolosky. Since she had fainted, he didn't realize this—or he might have tried another shot. Everyone was relieved with Linda's luck, but the task force recognized some new and very disturbing changes in Dart Man. He made no attempt to shoot Linda in the behind. In fact, he shot at her point-blank with the same type of dart he used on Lurleen Adams.

His symbols were changing.

Benton and Luther were first on the scene. Once they heard the description, there was no question in their minds that it was Dart Man. Linda Wolosky, though under care of a doctor, was able to ID the composite drawing they showed her. Luther found the dart in a wall directly behind where Linda had fainted. It was easy to find. All they had to do was look on the floor beneath where a small crater of plaster had been knocked out.

The task force hit the area hard and found that the perp would have had an easy time getting into the building where Wolosky lived. He must have known all along where she lived. It was a fairly posh building and had a two-way phone system in the lobby, but not everyone used it. All he had to do was ring buzzers until someone buzzed him in. Then he waited until Linda Wolosky showed up.

Benton and Luther found evidence, in the form of cigarillo butts, that he had waited a long time. There were five butts on the floor. Even for a chain smoker, that meant almost an hour of waiting. He was determined, Benton thought. No, psychotic was more like it.

Two people reported seeing a man outside the building who answered the description, but no one saw him leaving. One tenant had come into the hall after Linda Wolosky had screamed, but the man, an ex-cop, did not see anyone.

At the end of the day, the task force held a meeting at One Police Plaza. They wanted to get a clear idea where they were going and what their future plans were. Ellen Stevens also attended.

Nothing was said about the pressure on them to solve the case. That was understood. In its simplest terms, they were dealing with a potential murderer.

After two hours of brainstorming, they were no more near collaring Dart Man than they had been when he was using sewing needles.

"We have to come up with a new approach," Jim Frey said, "and fast."

Colleen McKay was sitting in the back of the room. For a few moments, as the task force had discussed where they were and where they were going, Colleen's mind wandered back to the moment in the garage when she came face-to-face with this psychopath.

She might come up against him again, she thought, when she least expected it. He had the advantage.

She raised her hand and stood up. "I have an idea that might help us," she said. "Actually, it's Jim's idea."

Many faces were turned toward her. Good ideas were valued.

"I think we should go back to the decoy idea," she said. "Set up a decoy in a situation that will suck this guy in."

"Who would be the decoy?"

"Me."

There was a ripple of surprise.

Frey waved his hand.

"I don't think so, Colleen," he said. "With all due respect to your talents and your guts, I think that is a bad idea. You don't have any police training, and what if it leads to a situation where you're not covered? Where are you? It's a good idea, but it's a job for a trained decoy. We have lots of people who can do this—and do it well."

"Maybe," Colleen said, "but what if this guy spots the decoy as just that? What if you dress someone like me and he finds out? What happens then? What will that trigger?"

Frey turned toward Ellen Stevens, but she looked at him blankly. He sensed that something was wrong. Frey then put the question to the rest of the task force. A few objected to using Colleen, but most thought it might work, that something radical was needed.

One cop asked, "How are we going to lure this guy to you, Colleen?"

"Well," she said, "based upon our understanding of him, as supplied by Dr. Stevens, we could goad him into coming after me. I could say something in a press conference that was denigrating. What do you think, Doctor?"

Ellen Stevens looked at Colleen. She took a moment to answer. Her voice had the slightest edge to it.

"I'm against this," she said, "for a couple of reasons. First, it rubs against my sense of ethics to have someone use my insights about a person as part of a police operation. I mean I'm not violently opposed, but it does bother me.

"Second, while you might be able to draw him out, he may well succeed in hurting you. I would have trouble dealing with that, because what I've given you would have made it possible."

"I can understand your concerns, Doctor," Colleen said, "but what is the alternative? If we don't do this, then he could kill someone who wouldn't stand a chance. Linda Wolosky was lucky," she added, "but the next victim may not be."

Ellen nodded. "I can see your point. I'm just having trouble with it."

Benton had listened carefully to the exchange, and he understood and respected both points of view.

He much admired Ellen for presenting views that were not popular with this group. However, he agreed with Colleen, and would tell Ellen so later. He had been a cop a long time, and over the years, the finer points of ethics and morality became secondary. "Take a liberal to a hundred crime scenes," the expression went, "and on the hundred and first he'll become a conservative."

There was silence, and then Frey settled it.

"We should go for it, but I think we should be in agreement. Those for Colleen doing this, please raise your hands."

Almost everyone in the room, Benton included, raised their hands. It was not necessary to take a nay vote.

CHAPTER 38

The PC reluctantly approved the use of Colleen McKay as a decoy, but he wanted to be privy to all the security measures taken.

Colleen was fitted for a Kevlar vest, which she was instructed she should wear all the time, since no one knew when Dart Man would strike again.

Colleen listened to the advice carefully—it came from Ellen Stevens, who felt obligated to get further involved, despite her misgivings about the overall idea.

Colleen was also wearing a body mike, which would allow her to communicate with the cops who would be watching her all the time, except when she was inside One Police Plaza. But even then, when she was in the garage, the cops would be there. There would be cops on the streets, cops following her home, and cops posted inside and outside her building. A policewoman was to stay there all the time.

Anyplace Colleen expected to be was carefully screened before she got there. For example, before she got home, her entire building and the surrounding area were gone over to make sure they were clean.

The PC had pulled all the stops out on this one. He wanted Dart Man stopped, once and for all.

The PC's office called a press conference at which Colleen McKay would make an announcement and she and the PC would answer any and all questions the media had.

The meeting was well-attended by the press, and Colleen lowered the bait into the water.

"I am happy to announce, ladies and gentlemen, that Linda Wolosky, the woman who was attacked by this—" She made what appeared to be a slip of the tongue. "—pip-squeak . . . I mean, individual, is doing fine."

"Are you afraid of this guy coming back at you?" asked a reporter friend of Colleen's, as they had previously arranged.

"Not really," Colleen said, "I'm not afraid of him. He hasn't proven anything, except that he's a cowardly thief in the night. But that's just my personal opinion."

* * *

That night, Colleen McKay, sweating due to the soft body armor under her suit, went through the ritual of going home.

She couldn't see any cops, but she knew they were there . . . and she was glad that they were. She felt, now more than ever, that Dart Man would strike again—and she would be the target.

About the time Colleen McKay was leaving One Police Plaza, Ellen Stevens and George Benton were in their apartment on Pelham Bay Parkway. Ellen was sitting by the kitchen window, George at the table. They knew that Colleen's sarcastic comments about Dart Man had been picked up by all the local news shows. If Dart Man was watching TV, he was bound to see it. They had not had a chance to discuss anything about the case. Benton took a deep breath and began.

"How are you doing?"

"I'm okay," Ellen said, "but I still have regrets about all this."

"I'm sorry I had to go against you, but I just . . . it's the way I felt."

Ellen turned and smiled. "That's okay, George. I'm glad you spoke your mind rather than just agreeing with me."

Benton nodded. "I based my decision on the victims. It may be intellectually empty, just an emotional response, but there it is. I've just seen too much."

"I can understand that," Ellen said. "This is not so simple. What if somebody gets killed and I had stopped this decoy plan by talking to the PC? Somebody would be dead. I wonder how I'd live with that."

Benton nodded. "I know, but right now we're both worried about Colleen. She could get hurt."

"I know."

"If this guy gets past the security they've got on her, it'll be a wonder," Benton said.

"Don't forget, he is desperate to get to her. And desperate men take chances."

"Sometimes I wonder," Benton said, "why people bother being born. It's so hard sometimes."

Ellen came over to him.

"It's the times between the sometimes that make it worthwhile," she said as she grabbed him around the waist, then kissed him on the lips.

Colleen McKay's nerves were frazzled by the time she arrived at her apartment. She was greeted by Meg, her police bodyguard.

Colleen thought of something and grimaced. She had hoped Dart Man would come soon. Who in their right mind would want that?

CHAPTER 39

For almost a day Frankenstein noodled over what the latest caper meant. Then they decided if anyone knew who was doing the latest jobs, it would be one of the

Gazza brothers or their confederates, or perhaps the fence, Irwin the Large.

They decided to try to do it by the book, so they began by contacting Irwin the Large's lawyer, a guy named Larry Fratelli.

They visited him at his office and told him what they were after. They wanted Irwin the Large to give them any information he might have on who did this latest crash-and-dash caper, and who whacked Slim Roberts. Frankenstein thought it might be the same people, but they had no motive and no leads.

Fratelli was a thin man who wore an expensive suit and many rings upon his manicured hands. He said, "I'm afraid that Mr. Gold doesn't know anything."

"How do you know that?" Stein asked.

"Mr. Gold has been given virtual immunity by the government for testifying against the Gazzas. I'm sure he would not want to get further involved."

"I see," Piccolo said, "since it can't do him any good, he doesn't give a fuck."

Fratelli shook his head. "It's not that," he said, "but I'm not at liberty to explain."

Frankenstein went at him a little longer but with no results. Irwin the Large was going to remain mute.

Frankenstein decided to take the bull by the horns. The next day they went to the Metropolitan Correctional Center to pay a surprise visit on Anthony Gazza.

The prison, commonly known as MCC, housed a wide variety of prisoners who couldn't make bail, or who were denied bail.

They had no idea if Anthony Gazza would see them, but it was worth a shot.

Anthony Gazza would see them.

As he came into the visitors' room, Anthony Gazza didn't seem to be a desperate character. He was a good-looking kid, even without his flowing black hair, which had been "trimmed" by the MCC butcher who masqueraded as a barber.

They sat down opposite him at a battered wood bench.

He was handsome, Stein thought, but there was a certain light in his eyes. A certain out-to-lunch light.

"We bring some very bad news," Stein said, "about Slim."

Gazza looked at him.

"I'm afraid," Piccolo said, "that he's deceased."

"He was found," Stein added, "in the trunk of a car."

For a moment Gazza's eyes glazed over and there was a hint of sorrow. "What happened?"

"He was tortured and beaten to death," Piccolo said.

"When and where?"

"His car was in a parking lot at LaGuardia," Stein said. "He had been dead a few days before they found him—yesterday."

There was a silence. Bad guys and good guys had basic rules. Frankenstein had broken almost every rule in the book, but they didn't dump on anyone when a buddy went down.

"He was a soldier," Gazza said, "and he knew the risks." He smiled a little smile. His eyes went a little out of focus. "That doesn't mean that there won't be retribution. . . ." His eyes refocused. "What do you want with me? I can't believe that you just came here to tell me that."

"We thought you might know something that can help us track the hump that did this. And did you hear about the job at 188th and the Concourse?"

"Yes."

"That's your MO. Someone's using your MO."

"Why would I want to help you?"

Frankenstein's interest was at an all-time high, but they didn't show it. Now they were sure he knew something. And he might talk, but he could also just tell them to take a fucking hike.

"Justice."

"My people can handle justice," Gazza said.

"Maybe you can and maybe you can't. We fucking guarantee it, and if you don't believe that, do a little more research on us."

"I know who you are," Gazza said, "and I know all about you."

"Then you know," Piccolo said, "that we are men of our word."

"You two have a reputation as being nuts."

"Maybe," Stein said, "but we don't break our word."

Gazza paused. His eyes flickered slightly. He looked at Piccolo, then Stein.

"I could talk to you but it would have to be off-the-record, strictly theory."

"So nothing can be used against you in a court of law," Stein said.

"Right," Gazza said.

Frankenstein looked at each other, then back at Gazza.

"That's okay with us."

"And maybe you could put a good word in for my brother Angelo."

"Why not you?" Stein asked.

"I'm the leader . . . the captain. It's bad form for the ship to go down and for the captain not to be on it."

Frankenstein nodded.

"Slim's killer," Gazza said, "and the guy who did the job on 188th Street, is probably Neil Falco—Junior."

"Neil's kid?"

Gazza nodded.

"Why?"

"He came to us and said he wanted in on our operation. That they were entitled to a piece of anything that went down in the city. And that we knew his name and we knew what that meant."

"What'd you tell him?"

"I said we had worked hard to build this thing. And the only people entitled to anything were our relatives when we died."

"What'd he say?"

"He was pissed. He's a leg-breaking macho guinea, no offense intended."

"None taken," Piccolo said.

"And that was it?" Stein said.

Gazza nodded and added, "So you're wondering why I still think it was him?"

"You took the words right out of my mouth," Piccolo said.

"Neil, Junior was really impressed with our operation, said he had researched us. Knew that jobs were very well researched and planned six months ahead. We even knew when the marks farted. Planning was everything. Execution was a piece of cake when we did our homework."

"I still don't understand," Stein said.

"He wanted to get his hands on our list of potential jobs. Don't forget, we never got caught."

"And who knew the list?"

"The whole gang. Including Slim."

Everything fell into place for Frankenstein. Neil, Jr. had worked Slim over for the "list" of potential jobs, and then killed him.

"How many jobs were involved?"

"Twenty, tentatively. We always fine-tuned the research. You learn that the hard way. On one of our first jobs the proprietor turned out to be a young and very well-armed retired cop. We were lucky to get out alive, and so was the ex-cop."

"We understand," Piccolo said.

"You asked me what I know—that's it."

There was a pause.

"How did you know where we were that night you collared us? No one had touched us for years. How did you know about Irwin the Large?"

"We got a tip."

"From who? Never mind, I know who. The Falcos."

"Neil Falco, Senior tipped us. We had a deal. It sounds like Junior was told to find your fence, and he saw what a nice operation you had. Then he went for your throat."

"That makes sense," Gazza said.

Frankenstein stood up.

"Anything else?"

Gazza shook his head.

"Okay, thanks. You never know how one hand washes the other," Piccolo said.

"If you arrest Junior, try to send him here, okay?"

Piccolo looked at him and smiled. This, he thought, is one tough piece of work.

CHAPTER 40

Frankenstein sat at the kitchen table in their apartment—otherwise known as command central—and thought about how they were going to go after Neil Falco, Jr. It was one thing to know he was guilty, and it was another to nail him. He wasn't just any hump. He had his father's considerable resources behind him.

"For openers," Stein said, "we could tell the old man that we think his son did the job on 188th Street and that wasn't our deal."

"And what, ask him to have the kid stop?" Piccolo asked.

Stein nodded.

"It's a dumb idea."

"You're right," Stein said.

"When these wops aren't whacking each other, blood is thicker than water. He won't care. He might even be proud of the kid."

"So what are we going to do?"

"I don't know," Piccolo said, "maybe just shadow the kid. Try to cop his ass in the act."

"You think he's involved in the jobs himself?"

"Sure," Piccolo said, "according to Remo, it fits his character."

Remo Aliperti was an NYPD detective and an expert on the Mafia. He told them that Neil, Jr. was a sadist and a crazy who liked to do his own work.

"He likes to kill," Aliperti had said, "and he always does the job himself. We got him tied into about twenty homicides. He was thirteen when he had his first kill. A very bad actor, just like his father."

"If we want to shadow this guy, we're not going to get any help from Bledsoe," Stein said. "The only thing that will make him happy is a collar."

"You're right."

"So we could shadow the guy . . . selectively."

"What do you mean?" Piccolo asked.

"Look at the Gazza MO. The jobs always go down after the stores close. We could try to shadow Falco after that."

"That's a good idea," Piccolo said, "and we could do it on our own time."

Frankenstein told Lawless of their plan, and he said he would arrange their tours so they could do it.

"I'll tell Bledsoe that you're working a new angle if he asks me. Otherwise, we won't say anything."

"Okay."

"I appreciate you guys doing this," Lawless said, "but that's why you're such good cops."

Frankenstein respected few people, and Lawless was one of them. They basked in the glow of his compliment and hoped they could catch that motherfucker on the next caper.

CHAPTER 41

Dart Man heard Colleen McKay call him a pip-squeak. It affected him as it had when Lurleen Adams called him that.

Colleen McKay would pay. He would show her what he was and what he could do.

He briefly considered getting a shotgun, but he decided the air rifle would teach her a lesson. If he hit her in the right place, she would be sorry.

He decided that the right place was her eye. He couldn't shoot her from a distance. If he held the muzzle against her eye and pulled the trigger, he would not miss.

Now he had to make up a plan to get her when she least expected it. Maybe he would be waiting for her in her garage. No, she would be expecting him. She might have someone with her. He might get caught. Maybe he could shoot her while she was stopped at a light.

Then he had an idea that he really liked.

After she parked in her garage, he would sneak in the backseat of her car and wait for her till morning.

But what if it was locked? What would he do then?

He couldn't break into it.

He knew what to do. He had seen it in a movie once. The monster had waited for the man under a car. When she came down, he could come out from under the car and shoot her.

She wouldn't be expecting it. He would prove how superior he was.

He fingered his groin.

CHAPTER 42

Dart Man walked slowly up 178th Street and Hillside Avenue. He knew the police were looking for a man with bushy hair, so he'd had his hair cut short.

He had decided that a rifle was too dangerous to carry on the street. A cop could come up to him and ask him what was in the carpeting, and he would have to show him the rifle.

It was much better to carry an ice pick, which he had taken from his aunt Martha's kitchen. It would do the job quite nicely. He would drive it into her eye, which was plump and round and whorish, just like her ass. She would never see again.

He turned on 178th Street and started to walk up Wexford Terrace.

It was late at night, so the cars would be few and far between.

He wouldn't go into the garage now. He would wait until morning when the garage door opened to let a car out. It would be easier to slip in unnoticed.

He walked up Wexford Terrace. In the distance the big cream-colored building where Colleen McKay lived loomed against a maroon sky. He still believed what he had been taught as a little boy, that a maroon sky meant it was going to rain the next day.

He crossed the street, since he disliked the idea of walking past the building.

He had just crossed when a cop car came into view. His stomach lurched and he had the urge to run. But he did not, since that would be very suspicious.

He made a sharp left into the doorway of a building almost directly across the street from the building where she lived. He could see the police car, but he could not be seen.

It seemed to be slowing down. Maybe it spotted him.

It stopped near the concrete ramp that led to the garage.

From the shadows, a man materialized.

What was going on?

The shadowy figure walked over to the cop car. What did he have in his hand?

A walkie-talkie.

Dart Man stepped farther back into the doorway.

It was a trap. The motherfucking bitch had set a trap. She thought she could catch him. She thought he was small and stupid.

His small hand slipped inside his pocket and he gripped the fat wooden stock of the ice pick, whose tip was stuck in a piece of cork. He gripped it so hard that when he released his fingers they hurt.

He was walking away when he heard the shouting and he knew he was in bad trouble.

"Hey! Wait a minute! Wait!" the cops yelled.

He took a few more steps and then broke into a dead run. A moment later he heard the screeching of tires and the wailing of a siren.

He ran for his life.

Forty-five minutes later he exited from the subway at Times Square.

It was a cool night, but he was bathed in sweat. He looked as if he had fallen into a lake.

He was scared, and very, very angry.

He walked along. The streets were virtually empty, and he was on the prowl. He needed to find someone.

He found someone.

She was an old homeless lady, maybe sixty-five. It was hard to tell with the homeless.

She was sleeping in the doorway of a liquor store.

He approached her. The smell of urine was strong.

He drove the ice pick into her chest with all the strength he could muster, and he didn't stop until the base of the stock pounded against her rib cage.

CHAPTER 43

Frankenstein knew that it would be very difficult maintaining surveillance on Neil Falco, Jr. This punk was raised in the Mafia. He could smell cops following him.

This is why Frankenstein thought it was good that they were following him only part-time. Junior would be less suspicious.

They used vans, all plain-looking and likely to be forgotten.

They decided not to follow him if he went anywhere on foot. Junior had been there when Frankenstein met with Neil, Sr., and he might recognize them.

Much of Neil Falco, Jr.'s life was devoted to making his muscles bigger. The first four days, he went to a gym every day and worked out for over an hour.

He also had an active nightlife, and seemed to have a steady quiff. He went out with one blonde three of the four nights they watched him.

Frankenstein didn't stay with him the whole night. They usually wrapped it up around nine, since they figured if he was going to rob a store, he would already have done it.

Each night he made a trip to his father's social club on Mulberry Street, probably to kiss a little ass.

On the fifth night he did something different. He went out alone to a bar in Brooklyn called Tommy's, located on Florio Street in the Bay Ridge section not far from the Verrazano-Narrows Bridge in an area filled with the Mafia.

Like the Arthur Avenue area in the Bronx, Bay Ridge was unchanged, untouched by crime or the intrusion of different ethnicities, because of the presence of wise guys. Blockbusting blacks or felons would end up in cellars without their cocks, so they tended to leave Bay Ridge alone.

Junior seemed furtive as he went into the neighborhood bar/restaurant. "I'll bet this fuck is making plans now," Piccolo said to Stein.

"I wouldn't bet against it."

They stayed with him until he left the bar alone, and went home to his daddy's house in Rockaway.

Frankenstein didn't follow him into the Rockaways, a beach community with quite a few year-round families. There were too many wise guys around who might eyeball them.

Junior went back to Tommy's two nights later, and Frankenstein sat in a van for three hours about a block away.

"Nothing's going to happen tonight," Piccolo said. "It would have happened already."

"Yeah," Stein said, "we might as well take a powder."

As they were about to leave, Piccolo, who was driving, noticed that a black Cadillac had pulled up behind them. Its lights were on and it was running. They couldn't see who was in the car.

"Howie, we got company."

Both men pulled their guns, Howie a 9mm Glock and Piccolo a .357.

A young black-haired guy dressed in black pants and a white shirt got out of the Cadillac. Piccolo thought he looked like a guinea bomb thrower.

He came up to the driver's side window.

Piccolo looked at him. He had bad skin, a big nose, and shifty eyes. Looked like a real humpknuckle.

"He wants to see you," the guy said.

"Who?"

"He's in the car."

Piccolo got out of the car.

"Why don't you stay back here," he said to Stein.

"You got it, partner," Howie said.

Piccolo walked toward the Cadillac with the .357 carried just behind his right thigh. Howie had gotten out of the car and stood behind it. He was ready to go.

The door opened and Piccolo got an unpleasant surprise.

Neil Falco, Jr. got out of the car. Two other guys got out with him. Including the original hump who approached Frankenstein, there were four in all. Piccolo noted their relative locations.

Junior sauntered up to Piccolo. He was smiling.

"Why the fuck are you guys following me?"

Piccolo said nothing.

"What are you trying to do? Catch me doing something naughty?"

It got a big laugh.

"I ain't done nothin' bad," he said, "so stop fucking following me."

Piccolo said nothing. He motioned to Howie to join him. Howie started walking toward him.

"If you don't stop following me, I'm going to send my daddy after you," Junior said.

This got another big laugh. Junior turned to go back to the car.

"I got something for you," he said as Howie joined Piccolo.

Junior took something from his pocket and offered it to Piccolo. When Piccolo didn't take it, Junior dropped it on the ground. It looked like a diamond ring.

Junior laughed and turned back to the car.

Piccolo spoke for the first time.

"Your bimbo girlfriend takes it up the ass from gorillas," he said.

Junior started to walk back toward Piccolo. Piccolo smiled and so did Howie. Junior stopped and pointed at Piccolo.

"You got a dirty mouth," he said, "you should wash it out."

"You want to wash it for me?"

Neil smiled and wagged his finger at Piccolo, and then he and his goons piled into the car and pulled away with tires burning rubber.

* * *

Later, in their apartment, Piccolo consoled himself with wine. Howie was drinking his San Pellegrino, his dieting temporarily shelved.

On the table lay the diamond ring.

"He was sticking this up our ass," Piccolo said, "and giving us a message. A message that reads fuck you."

"That's right," Howie said. "Up ours with gauze. He knows we know he was behind the latest caper—and that he's going to do more. No question in my mind."

"This guy really pisses me off," Piccolo said. "How about you?"

"Yeah, I'd like to neutralize him."

"We can."

"We can? How? He's on to us."

"There is a way," Piccolo said. "Trust me. Bernice Allen is the way."

"Huh?" Stein said.

"Trust me," Piccolo said, and he quaffed his wine and gave Howie a big gap-toothed smile.

Chapter 44

The homeless woman who had been ice-picked by Dart Man was known by the name "Becky." Doctors figured her to be about seventy years old.

Everybody, including Becky, was lucky.

Becky—And Dart Man—had been spotted by some tourists, who had run screaming to the police. So it was not long between the time she was stabbed and was being admitted to ICU at St. Claire's Hospital.

The ice pick had gone deep, but it had missed her vital organs. Though it was a severe wound, she should recover.

The task force, the mayor, the PC, Benton, and Ellen breathed a collective sigh of relief at this news. Though it could not be confirmed, it seemed for sure that the stabbing was Dart Man's response to what Colleen McKay had said.

It was decided that the task force would not play any more games. They would track him down with straight detective work. There would be no more unnecessary risks.

To some degree, Ellen felt responsible for the violence done to Becky, but she knew there was little to be gained by gnashing her teeth. Life was like that. She just had to move on.

The task force was feeling depressed, though no one said it. The reasons were simple. They hadn't captured Dart Man. Now he had attempted murder and was bound to murder someone if they didn't catch him.

George Benton was much more disturbed than he revealed to anyone, including Ellen. He felt the assault was his fault because he had gotten Ellen involved, which ultimately led to the decoy operation. He felt badly because he couldn't crack the case. And he also found himself struggling with the old insecurity that had plagued him when he met Ellen.

He realized that this was illogical, but he couldn't change the way he felt.

There was one good thing about insecurity. It drove you long after other people had given up.

Benton stayed home and scrutinized the Dart Man file, which was quite a thick document. He was searching for a detail that would lead him somewhere.

He had worked until the wee hours of the morning and had only come up with one thing that had any potential. The smell. If they could identify the sweet scent that both Colleen and Linda Wolosky had reported, maybe they could trace a purchase back to Dart Man. A small black man buying cologne might be remembered.

He decided to catch a few hours of sleep and make some calls in the morning.

When he got up, he immediately called Linda Wolosky.

Linda had smelled it, but she had no idea what it was. It did smell like perfume, but she had no idea what kind. She could not add anything to what she had already told him.

Colleen was able to narrow the scent down to some degree. "It was perfume, but I have no idea what kind. I use many perfumes, and I've never smelled it."

Benton asked her if she could spare some time to go to a perfume counter—say Saks Fifth Avenue—and try to identify it. She said she could make it that day.

When Ellen got up, she didn't say much to George. She knew nothing she could say would do much good. He had to see this through to the end.

So she just went over to him and wrapped her arms around him and said, "I love you."

He hoped she always would.

CHAPTER 45

Colleen McKay and Benton were standing at the perfume and notions counter at Saks Fifth Avenue trying to explain what they were looking for to the manager. She had an interesting suggestion.

"Why don't you try some offbeat perfumes?"

So, Colleen began sniffing perfumes that were not popular or commonplace.

Colleen identified the scent of the third perfume she smelled, something called Roue.

"You're sure," Benton said.

"Definitely."

Benton questioned the manager about this particular perfume. She knew it well. It was imported from France and was very expensive, and it was not a top seller in Saks.

"Do you know who distributes it?" Benton asked.

She gave them the name of an import-export company called Joe Frank and Associates.

"Do you have any idea how many stores carry this perfume?"

"Only the stores that appeal to a clientele that can afford it."

Benton thanked her, and before he and Colleen left he took a shot in the dark.

"Do you happen to remember," he said, "a small black man coming in and buying this perfume?"

"I don't remember anyone like that," the woman said.

So much for miracles.

Benton called the distributor, and found that the perfume was "manufactured" for distribution in this country by a firm called Benjamin Products. He was told that they distributed to some 150 retail outlets in the metropolitan area.

Benton hung up and left a note for Frey that the team should start canvassing the outlets to see if they could come up with someone who remembered selling perfume to a small, bushy-haired black man.

He then drove home to get a few more hours of sleep, since it was foolish to operate without sleep. He felt sure that Frey would want to begin canvassing.

He wondered what would possess a man who hated women to wear perfume. Was he gay? Was it a gas that protected him? What did it mean?

It could mean anything. He would ask Ellen about it when he saw her.

As he drove, he began to feel sleepy. He had to watch

it. He'd fall asleep and then all his insecurities would be put to rest for all time.

Why would he wear perfume?

He did not know.

He went by some factory areas and noticed smoke billowing from the stacks.

At least he had given up smoking, which was a bad-news habit for a hypochondriac. He imagined every puff to be the final insult to his bronchi, which would begin to sprout death flowers.

He was glad he had stopped.

Then he felt something click from deep within his mind.

Why did he assume that Dart Man was wearing the perfume?

After all, it was not just smokers who had that smoky smell. It could come from other people's tobacco. It clung to the clothes. . . .

Suddenly he was wide awake. He maneuvered the car into the next exit lane and sped back downtown.

Chapter 46

Benton got to Benjamin Associates at around three in the afternoon.

It was a typical factory in Long Island City, with one

exception. Few smelled like this. He could smell the scent of Roue in the lobby.

He showed his shield to the receptionist, and she called the manager, a nervous-looking man in his mid-fifties.

"I'm looking for a small black man with bushy hair that may or may not have been recently cut."

"We have a number of black people working for us. . . ." He paused. "We do have a security window," he said. "You can view the people on the line without them seeing you."

"Good."

Benton and the manager proceeded to the second floor and looked out over the bustling factory. The smell was not unpleasant, but intense.

He scanned the room and was halfway down a middle conveyer line when his eyes fixed on a small black man. Gooseflesh rose on his arms.

"May I use your phone?" Benton asked.

"Sure."

Benton made his call and returned to the security window to wait for backup and to watch Dart Man go about the business of making perfume.

His name was Stewart Childs, and he lived with his aunt.

The task force descended on his room, and what they found told them two important things.

They had the right man. They found darts, air guns, porno stuff, clips of the Dart Man attacks, needles, two straws, and paper feathers. And they had found him in the nick of time, for leaning in a corner of the closet was a brand new 12-gauge shotgun. Childs was very calm and mild when they arrested him, offering no resistance. He hardly seemed to be a man who would use a shotgun on people. Then again, that's how extremely violent people are described all the time.

CHAPTER 47

Neil Falco, Jr., was getting ready to do the job. They had a store in Manhattan lined up. It sold expensive mens' clothing, which meant they could be out with a hundred thousand dollars worth of stuff in just minutes.

Junior had gathered a gang of four to work with him, but he wasn't directly involved in this one. He knew those two fucking cops would be trying to get him, and he had to be careful. As much as he wanted to be on the job, he knew better.

At about six o'clock he decided to go to the gym and pump some iron and then go and see his squeeze, Connie. He smiled. He liked pumping iron, but he also liked pumping Connie.

He left the house and started his black Cadillac, which was parked across the street, with the remote control device Pop had given him for his birthday.

He let it warm up, then he got inside and headed for

the gym. He hardly noticed the black Trans Am that was about seventy-five yards behind him.

An hour and a half later, refreshed and showered, Junior exited the Powers Gym on West Eighth and strode to the parking garage down the block.

He walked down into the garage and paid his money to Sam, the black attendant. Sam seemed nervous.

He turned to go to his car, and was face-to-face with Frankenstein. Piccolo held a piece of paper delicately in one hand.

"Search warrant," Piccolo said.

"Hey, fuck you, fuck—"

Stein's fist smashed into Junior's face, knocking him to the ground. The duo proceeded to open the car without benefit of a key. Stein used a pry bar to snap locks and break windows.

Junior was enraged—and scared. He sat on the ground, feeling his jaw and wiping the blood off himself.

They seemed to know exactly where to look. Stein ripped out the backseat, and Piccolo reached in and removed something, then he turned and walked toward Junior.

"What's this?" Piccolo asked. He held up a baggy partly filled with gems.

"That's not mine! This is a fucking setup!"

"It looks like swag to me," Piccolo said. "Illegal proceeds from a crash-and-dash caper . . . a serious felony."

"No!" Falco screamed, "no!"

"Yes," Piccolo yelled, "yes . . ." and Stein chimed

in, "Yes . . . yes . . . yes . . ." Their voices echoed within the confines of the garage, and Junior knew he was dealing with men who were bonkers and very dangerous.

CHAPTER 48

The collar of Dart Man inspired an outpouring of adulation and commendation. Several days later, after the hubbub had subsided, George Benton sat in a restaurant with Ellen Stevens. They were having an after-dinner drink.

All night, George had seemed a little distracted.

"How's it going George?" she asked.

"Fine."

"No, really."

Benton looked at her. "Well," he said, "I sometimes wonder about myself. I feel sort of sorry for Dart Man. I know he was a potential killer and all, but he is no more responsible for his actions than is the man on the moon."

"I agree," Ellen said. "People like him are compelled to do what they do."

"I didn't tell you this, but in addition to the pornography and the guns, we found something else."

"What?"

"An old photo. I asked him who it was. He told me it was his mother."

Benton sipped his drink and smiled a little.

"The woman in the picture—his mother—was wearing a bathing suit. Can you guess what was the most prominent feature of her body?"

Ellen nodded.

"I asked if he was in touch with her, and he said no. I asked him when did you last see her, and he said 'I don't remember.'" George's eyes misted. "Isn't that sad?"

They were silent for a moment. Ellen reached over and touched George's hand.

"I was thinking about how lucky I am," he said. "Childs will go into the system and be screwed over until the day he dies. Me? I have a chance for a life. I'm in therapy and I have a woman who loves me. It seems so unfair."

"That's only because it is, George," she said. "But maybe there's a grand design. Maybe in the end it will make some kind of sense. Maybe people like Stewart Childs and all the rest can go to a better place than this."

"Yes," Benton said, "yes."

Chapter 49

Frankenstein entered the Falco social club on Mulberry Street a week after the collar of Neil Falco, Jr. They were there at the request of Falco, Sr.

This time, they were frisked before entering the back room. What Falco was going to say to them he didn't want recorded.

They were ushered in by the same pockmarked guy as before.

The air in the back room was considerably chillier than it had been before, and it had nothing to do with the heating system.

Neil Falco, Sr. was looking at them.

"Sit down, gentlemen," he said. "Care for something to drink?"

They shook their heads.

He sat down and looked at them. He looked displeased.

"Look," he said, "I'm a little bent with you guys. This is a fucking bullshit rap. You set him up."

"He's guilty," Piccolo said, "no matter."

"Those diamonds weren't from the job he pulled. They were planted."

"He's guilty," Piccolo said, and from his tone Falco realized that he would not say any more.

"Look, can we make a fucking deal?"

"No," Piccolo said. "Did you know he whacked someone?"

"Who?"

Stein explained about Slim.

"There's no fucking proof, is there?"

Frankenstein looked at each other. They didn't even know why they were talking to this hump. Maybe just to bust his chops.

"I'm fucking telling you right now," Falco said, "I am very fucking displeased with this."

Frankenstein said nothing for a moment.

"I'm going to take that as a threat," Piccolo said, "and I want to say something to you, the same thing I said to that fat fuck of a wop motherfucker Capezzi down in Philly when we had a squabble with him. We play the fucking game basically like Colombians. If either of us gets killed, then the other will pursue the killer and their fucking colleagues and their families all the way. And there are no fucking rules."

"Your son did not honor our deal," Stein said. "He went behind our backs. It makes you wonder what he'll do next. My advice is to let him do his time. It's the better fucking way."

Piccolo's brow furrowed. "Hey, Howie, you used a curse word."

They got up and left. Falco watched them leave, his face considerably whiter than when they had arrived.

* * *

Frankenstein entered Allen's jewelry store on 188th Street off the Concourse. It was already being renovated.

Bernice Allen was standing in the store, supervising the carpenters and other tradesmen.

"How you doing?" Piccolo asked.

"Good, Frank."

"Spoke to the DA a little while ago. Everything is going great. Just wanted to thank you again, and to say that they expect the trial to go down in two months, and you'll get your diamonds back then."

"Good," she said, "score one for the good guys."

"You got it. And thanks very much. We need more citizens with chutzpah like you."

"Hey Frank, I was once a cop. I know how the game is played."

They left.

As they walked, they were relaxed. They were not waiting to be whacked. They knew they wouldn't be, because Falco knew they were men of their word. A few years in prison for his son would be better than spending the rest of his life in the bone orchard.